Those Small Lil

In Life and Lo

Those Small Lil Things

In Life and Love

Rahul Saini

Srishti
PUBLISHERS & DISTRIBUTORS

SRISHTI PUBLISHERS & DISTRIBUTORS
N-16 C. R. Park
New Delhi 110 019
srishtipublishers@gmail.com

First published by Srishti Publishers & Distributors in 2008
Second impression, 2009
Copyright © Rahul Saini, 2008

ISBN: 81-88575-69-0

Typeset in AGaramond 11pt. by Suresh Kumar Sharma at Srishti

Printed and bound in India

For all those simple charms, that led me to write this story.

Laaaaave wiiiiiiill find a wayyyyyy.

– Kabhi alvida na kehna.

What they have to say.

Pragati — Raj? Really? He wrote a book? Mentioning me? Ok. I cant really recall any Raj from my kindergarten... But it's nice to know. Funny how you can affect someone's life so much, without even knowing...

Vani — I don't know... I do remember him. We had a class photo clicked that year. It's just that he was always a little... weird, always.

Mona — Raj. Yes I do remember him. I heard he is an architect now. He was a nice guy then. But it's very overwhelming to know. He remembered all the tiny little details of everything... all those time... I feel ...I don't know...honoured?

Neelhans — He is gal crazy. And a liar. It's not right, but its ok you know. No girl can ever be happy with him. Coz one girl is never enough for him. But I have grown out of it. And O! I got my haircut, see. O no no, its not coz of him that I got my hair cut! .

Shilpa — O Raj! Oooo! He finally wrote it! Good. He is a gem of a person. Almost saintly. Although we used to talk a lot about getting married back then but he never looked at me as that would make me uncomfortable you know. And about marrying him, I take life as it comes you know, never plan. Lets see where life takes me.

Ishika — Hmm. he is a very selfish and self-centered man. Even in bed. I would have loved to tell you more about him, but... I am getting late. I am going to meet someone you know... and please, we are *not* going around!

Pragya – O Raj! He is the sweetest! He is my sweet heart! I love him the most. And you know something, he can dance!

Aksha – We are still very good friends. And he handled the whole situation very well. I can imagine no one else who could have done it better.

Boss – Raj! Yes he used to work in our office. I tried so hard to teach him the ways of the world but, (he sighs). Never mind. He is a very bright chap. (smiles brightly) he was my favourite.

Part 1

Part 1

What he has to say

Prologue.

Hi!

"*Hum ek baar jeetay hain, ek hi baar marte hain, ek hi baar shaadi karte hain, aur pyaar, pyaar bhi ek hi baar karte hain*" Rahul told his mother, who looked back at him, eyes half filled with tears. I was in 9th std, when I saw it for the first time *Kuch Kuch Hota Hai*, and I think, it was, after watching Rahul, Anjali and Tina's eternal love story* for the third time that I started to think about this particular dialogue. I didn't really agree with Shah Rukh there. The point being, I don't think that if you lose one love, you can never fall in love again.

I watch a lot of movies, and when I say a lot, I mean, A LOT. I

---

* Ha ha ha ha! Yes, some people do think like that!

learn a lot from them too. This also I must have learned from some movie only, (that one learns a lot from movies). Many people laugh at me for watching so many movies, my present boss has many times tried to tell me that. Today only during lunch he told me, when I asked him if he had seen *Chicago*. He said, "I have my priorities very clear, I don't sacrifice work for movies." dabbing his lips with a napkin. And it was funny coz when I first heard him, I thought he said, I HAVE MY PRIORITIES VERY CLEAR, I DON'T SACRIFICE MY MOVIES FOR MY WORK**. Anyways, I still asked, "but everyone does come across some movie or the other at some point of time or the other." I mean like come on!!! Who would have not seen *Chicago*?!! LIKE *WHO*?! (By the way, if any of you have not seen it, put this book down this instant, go rent / buy a vcd / dvd and watch the movie first. You are not doing justice to yourself if you have not seen that movie yaar! It's one of the greatest musicals of all times!!!)

Anyways, before we go any further, I must tell you a few things about myself. I am a quarter century old, and think I have already been in love like eight times, (excluding the present one). And like most of the twenty five year olds, four days out of seven, I crib my life sucks! My job sucks! My boss is the king of the KINGDOM OF ALL DEVILS! I am very lonely! Etc. etc. etc. Am an architect by profession. AND I LOVE TELLING PEOPLE THAT! FULL STOP! I watch almost every movie that is released; listen to music eighteen hours out of twenty-four. I come from the small town of Jalandhar where everyone and everything is so peaceful and calm and serene and SLOWWWW that NOTHING BLOODY MOVES AT ALL!!! And the people there know how to swear and use words like bhain@#*#, maa@$^* and all like the air they breathe!!! Uuuuhhhhhhhh! Sorry,

---

** Coz that is how I function.

4

must not lose my temper, Must count twenty! One, two, three, four, five hmm done. Ok.

So what was I telling you? Yes! I am basically a Punjabi by nature AND MY ENGLISH SUCKS. BUT I WILL STILL BLOODY WRITE THIS BOOK!!!! AAAAAAAAA! Sorry must count to ten. Hmm ok, done. Hmm, so, I have done my schooling and everything from Jalandhar itself. It was only when I joined college that I actually stepped out of the city for the first time.

Anyways, I want to tell you about all of my eight love stories. Let's start with the first one.

I am named and I fall in love for the first time.

I still remember the day I was named. I had turned three – old enough to be put in school. Every thing had been settled; the school authorities and the principal etc. had been approached correctly to make sure that I was admitted to the best nursery school in the city. All arrangements had been. All but one – MY NAME! Till then I was called BAWA. I was offered a choice between Raj and Rahul. I chose Rahul I was fascinated with the name. I really loved it, for what reason I really don't know, but really loved it. Anyways, that is the day that I was named, I was named Raj. If they were not to listen to me why did they ask me what I liked better in the first place? But it was ok; I settled for being Raj in my real life and Rahul in my dreams. Hmm, so there I was, with a new name – Raj, fully aware of the fact that I was the cutest kid on earth, marching to my new school. Completely unaware of the fact who I was gonna meet there – the first love of my life – Pragati.

I still remember her very clearly. The memory of her face still doesn't fail to bring a smile. Her face… it was soo perfect and …round, …that it looked… just, exactly, like a …nice , round, white, tempting chapati. I don't really remember exactly how we first met but I recall that I really wanted to marry her. And that she was my best friend. And that we used to have loads and loads of fun. I don't remember now what we used to do together, but I do recall that we used to sit in class together and the teacher used to love to see us together. 'So lovely you two look together' she used to say. I don't know what we talked about, but that we talked a lot. I could not imagine life without her, school without her, anything in this world without her! I was crazy about her! Man, really, I was! She was the only person I would think about, *all day*. I crossed all limits in her love. And one of the worst things I did while I was in love with her was – developed a habit of writing her name with mine. Unaware about everything around me, deeply engrossed in her thoughts, picturing us together, I would tilt my head to one side very fondly, and write her name with mine, *everywhere*. And I once made one of the biggest mistakes ever, till date – scribbled her name with mine, ON MY DAD'S ACCOUNT BOOKS. I won't tell you much about the consequences, but lets just say that I almost died that day. And was reborn.

Anyways, so, time passed and we grew closer. Today, I remember only one conversation clearly with her. It went like this.

(That day, in school, we were taught that houses could be single storied, double storied, or triple storied and so on.)

'I have a double storied house.' I said.

'I have a tliple storied house.' She said.

I frowned.

'I have a vvvvery big garden in front of my house.' I said

' I don't have a vely big galden in flunt my house.' She said

I smiled.

'I have a loutyald in my house.' She said

'What is a loutyald?' I said

'It is a vely big loom with no loof.' She said

'Hmm, my house is better, all the rooms in my house have roofs.' I said

I smiled again, feeling very happy and satisfied as was completely convinced that my house was better that hers. And I did not feel bad for her for having an inferior house than mine coz I thought that she was anyways gonna come and live in my house with me when we grew up and got married. I knew quite a bit about marriage and stuff, my *bhua's* daughter had got married like 3 months before I was put to school. I also knew that if you go seven times round a fire with a girl, wearing wedding clothes, God gave you a baby as well. The conversation went on,

'Where is your house?' I said

'Its behind the petlol pump.' She said 'whel is youl house?'

'It is outside the school, my address is 255 Laj Pant Nagar Jalandar City.' I said

'Ok.' She said

'Ok.' I said

That's about all I remember of that conversation. And I remember very clearly that after that day, when my dad would come back from office, I would ask him every single day,

'Papa car main petrol dalvane chale?

At times dad would say we have enough petrol in the car. At which I would get very upset, and howl* and say that I wanted to go to the petrol pump. Sometimes he would take me for a ride to the petrol pump. At times, he would agree to go to the petrol pump to fill petrol in the car. On both occasion, I would keep looking out, *all the time.* There was a house behind the petrol pump that we used to go to, but I never saw her there. After a few days it struck me – she might me staying in a house, which was behind some other petrol pump! So I started asking my dad to go to some different petrol pump every evening. But sadly the search ended with no success.

Time passed, and the year came to an end. It was time to part – time to leave the nursery school. I didn't know what was going to happen. Without her company I felt life had come to an end. Only toys and ice cream would make me happy. I was sure that I was gonna turn into a Devdas when I grew up. I had seen the movie; it was in black and white. The guy was very good looking, fair and foreign

---

* Now you know why kids behave weirdly at times.

educated, just the way I used to picture myself when grown up. He was not able to be together with his love and started drinking a lot, developed a cough, which the doctors called "TV*" and died in the end. I had started believing that the same would happen to me, I had already developed a cough! (Without any drinking however.)

But you know what? Life goes on. The cough was cured within a week or so, I think. And my parents had already decided the school they were going to put me into next. All this whileI was just praying to God for one thing – 'O God please let Pragati be in the same school that I am gonna be put into.'

When I think about my first love story today, - I think that is where it ended. (But even today when we go to get our car fueled, I look around and wonder – could this be the petrol pump...)

** That is what I thought it was called, TV, and not TB.

I am told ki mujhe koi bhi ladki mil sakti hai and tiny girls run after me, screaming and calling me CHHAMAK CHHALLO!

"Maloon hai, tum agar chaho na, to tumhe koi bhi ladka mil sakta hai." Rahul said, his elbow resting on Anjali's shoulder, looking at her. Anjali looked up, her eyes filled with tears. Very softly she asked, "koi bhi?"

"Koi bhi." He snapped his fingers and pointed at her nose. "Koi bhi. Bus us ki ankhe kharab honi chahiyen."

"Stupid" she whispered, and gave Rahul a soft punch. Rahul hugged her.

I knew for sure what Kajol was going through, and why she was saying what she was saying. And I felt really bad for her. A heart ache is the toughest to bear. It was, I think only 2 days back, when I was talking to Rushi. She, is my present love interest by the way. And I have been trying to win her, for the past I think, 11 years now. If you really ask me, I don't see any chance, but I am still trying. I have proposed to her 3 times already. Only to be rejected, every-single-time. But I am not one of those who give up easily you know, I am a taurean, TO THE CORE! We are still friends. 😊😊

So, two days back, I had called Rushi to tell her that I had been proposed to by a girl! Yes, it happens. Now in India also. In real life. She is a really nice girl and everything but it's just that my heart is set on Rushi so much so that that I cannot think about any one else. So, I was telling her about how that girl feels about me and stuff and expressed amazement how any girl could like me. I am not good to look at, am as skinny as a starved dog, completely dumb and good for nothing. If at all I am good at anything, it is, I think, messing up every situation, which no one else can possibly

10

even imagine, could be messed up.

So I went on like- 'I fail to understand how a girl can possibly like me.'

And she was like *'Arre pagal aise nahi kehte.'*

And I was all 'What do you mean?'

And she *'Pagal,* any girl can like you."

'Any girl?' I asked

"Yes, any girl."

'Any girl?'

"Yes, any girl. And you know what? U ARE VERY STUPID! *NIKAMME*!!" She said laughing.

I didn't want to take it any further. I had already done it thrice. Last time was only eight months back, didn't want to repeat it so fast. I kept quiet. Then the conversation shifted to general topics of discussion weather, movies, books etc.

I will switch back to this story in a while, but for now, back to childhood.

So, I was put in this new school, the best convent in town – St. Joseph's Junior School. And Pragati was not there. She did not sit next to me any longer. I felt lonely, had no friends and would cry not to go to school every single morning. Till, till she came - Vani. Ummm O god…she was… gorgeous! She was very fair, very close to the colour of the pure white Pomeranian my neighbours had. She would always wrinkle her nose when she would talk. Even when she said "hi". I wanted to play with her in the games period. But she… she had some very weird friends, who used to bully me a lot. I can never forget. They were a group of three girls, Vani, Mona and Munmun. Munmun was the wickedest of them all. Mona was ok, but still dangerous. Vani was a doll. One day, during the recess, I was having my tiffin, sitting alone. Looking at Vani, wanting to talk to her. Suddenly Munmun appeared

11

in front of me out of nowhere! She stared right into my eyes and said, '*Kya baat hai chamak chhallo, bada chikna lag raha hai aaj?*' I got shit scared. I gulped. I mean what did she mean!!!! What was she gonna do next!!!! I had seen villains in the movies talking like that! Just then I heard another voice from the back, '*Kya hua mere chammak chhallo? Dar gaya kya?*'

It was Mona, and she pushed me from the back and I fell down. My tiffin box fell, on the ground. Munmun picked it up, showed it to me in a teasing manner, and said, "Do you want this?" And started running away. I ran after her, Mona and Vani ran after me. All three of them screaming, "*Chammak chhallo Chammak Chhallo!*"

I was a fast runner as a kid. I did manage to get my tiffin box back. But after that I cried. I cried very hard. IT WAS EMBARRASSING!!!

But it worked. Our class teacher got to know about the thing that happened. And she made Vani sit next to me in class!

We became friends. She had a very shrill voice, almost hurting to the ears. And I used to imitate her; (may be that's the reason why my voice is the way it is today, weird and shrieky).

It's very true what they say; good things come in small packages. Vani's dad was in the army, as soon as people started to identify us as …together, her father got his transfer orders. She left. And I was left alone! Again! I wanted to end everything. End going to school, end this world, END MY LIFE! I had seen *Qayamat se qayamat tak* some time around then. I wanted to kill myself, with a dagger, just like the Raj in the movie did in the end in the sunset. But I didn't. (And thank god!!!!!)

After she left there was silence, a long silence. That silence lasted for 3 long years, till I met Rushi.

My most wonderful office!

I HATE MY JOB!!!!! I HATE IT! I HATE IT! I HATE IT!!!!!!!!!
AAAAAAAAAA!!!!! Ok, no, wait, I must relax, chill, Count to 20. no,
50. 1,2,3,4,5, ,12,13, ,21,22,23, 35,36, 37, 48,49,50. Ok. Done.
Hmm, but seriously, I completely fail to understand, why is it this
hard for my boss to follow a little discipline, and let his employees
have the actual office working hours that he 'officially' declares! I
mean how hard is it to let people start working at 10 AM and let
them leave at 6.30 PM. It is *really* bugging and I am seriously losing
it. You know it is not my fault that people don't come to his office
to work, BUT TO LIVE THERE INSTEAD! IT IS NOT MY PROBLEM
IF PEOPLE IN HIS OFFICE ARE COMPLETE WORKAHOLICS AND
DO NOT HAVE ANY LIFE AT ALL!! I am soooo mad I can't even
explain!!! Its like if you try to leave office on time, everyone will look
at you as if you have just stepped out of the bathroom without any
clothes on!!!!!! Or your fly is open or something!!

It was an ok day at office, things were going fine, but only till my
wristwatch struck 6 in the evening. My phone rang. It was Aksha.
By the way, before I go any further I must tell you about my friends,
Aksha, Guneet and Shalini. These three girls constitute the core
group of my friends. And whether I like it or not, or whether I have
time or not, WE HAVE TO MEET. E-V-E-R-Y S-I-N-G-L-E E-V-E-N-I-
N-G!

It was Aksha on the phone. I was in the middle of a meeting with
my project leader, Shweta. She was going through the work I had
done in the past 3 hours and was pointing out as many mistakes as
possible, and giving me as much work as possible which I should
finish before I left. Yes all bosses are like that   EVIL! Anyways, I
received Aksha's call,

"Haeiiiiiii! *Kya haal?*"

'I am ok.'

"*Achha what's your shaam ka scene?*"

'Aksha I am still in office. In the middle of a meeting'

"Ok. So, how was your day?"

'Aksha I am busy, can't talk. Will call you in a while?' Shweta was giving me such angry looks, which would have killed Hercules! Like a raging bull she looked!

"Ok! Will be waiting for your call!"

'Ya, bye.'

"Take care, Baeeee!"

'Bye.'

Uff! Girls I tell you! GIRLS!

Anyways, it was 6 AND SHWETA HAD AGAIN GIVEN ME WORK, WHICH WOULD LAST 3 MORE HOURS!!!!! And on top of that I had all that haeiiiii baeeeeee business going in my head! My brain was about to explode. The meeting lasted for another fifteen minutes. After I got free from the meeting, I called Aksha.

'Hello'

"haeiii"

'Ya, hi'

"*Acha* listen, we all are reaching CCD in like an hour. Will be waiting there for you."

'Aksha I think I am busy. Won't be able to make it today.'

"whaeeeee?"

'Just got work for the next three hours.'

"What nonsense! You tell your boss you have some *very important work* to do. He can't make you work beyond office hours *everyday*!!"

14

She was right. And it was irritating, it's always irritating when you know that the other person is right and that you can't do anything about the situation you are stuck in.

'Ok. I will leave office in the next one hour.'

"No, half an hour Raj. HALF-AN-HOUR. HALF AN HOUR. HALF AN "

'Ok, ok, FINE! Half an hour.'

The half hour passed. And it was time for the real test, to pass the hall where boss and the other employees sat everyday. As soon as the clock struck 6.30, boss would sit up in his chair, with each and every muscle in his body all tensed, rotating his eyeballs all around, 360 degrees, like a chameleon, to check if anyone was leaving – if he needs to stop anyone.

I picked up my bag, took a deep breath, said all the prayers, and started walking. I was passing his chair, his back towards me; I was hoping he wouldn't see me. But he did. He saw my reflection in his computer screen. Yes, this was his way to keep an eye on everyone, in front of him *and* behind him. And then it happened! I heard,

"Raj, leaving so early?!"

I looked at my watch, it was 6.45. SIX FORTY-FIVE!

'Yes boss, I have to meet someone.'

"And you seem to be very excited about the meeting."

I stood silent. No expression.

"So, how was your day?" He asked, and I must tell you that when he speaks, he moves his hands in a very weird manner. Like he is doing some kind of an Indian classical dance or something. I never fail to hear sitar sounds whenever he talks to me.

'It was fine boss, it was good.'

"I was thinking of giving you a few sections to draft, but you seem to be in a hurry."

He looked at his watch. I looked at mine. It was 6.48.

"You know what, I am gonna leave in another 10 minutes, why don't you go with me. I will drop you'

"Boss... "

"You know what? You never say no to a free hitch. Go outside and wait, I will just come. Or you know what! Better still, you can draft a section in that time, maybe you *should* do that! Go draft the section, we will leave in 15 minutes."

I HATE HIM! I HATE MY BOSS! I HATE THIS WORLD! AND I HATE MYSELF!!!! AAAAAAAAAAAAAA!

I went back to my workstation, turned on my computer and started to work.

Another half an hour passed away. The phone rang again. It was Guneet. This was not a good sign. I gulped, and with my sweaty hands, I picked up my phone.

'Hello'

"YOU ARE A CHICKEN!!! A MOUSE!!!! YOU HEAR ME!!!! CHICKEN MOUSE!!"

'Hi Guneet' I said, forcing a reluctant smile on my face.

"I DON'T LIKE PEOPLE WHO CAN NOT STAND UP FOR THEMSELVES!"

"I was leaving but bo... "

"I HAVE SAID WHAT I WANTED TO, I DON'T WANT TO LISTEN TO ANYTHING. DON'T EVER TALK TO ME AGAIN!"

"but Sup..."

She hung up the phone.

BUT GUNEET PLEASE TRY TO UNDERSTAND! I felt like screaming my lungs out. But could not. BUT COULD NOT!!!!!!! AAAAAAAAAAAAAAAAAAAAAAAAA!!!!!!

Anyways, it was just the usual we-are-leaving phone call. So I didn't react. Just then the lights went out!!

God had answered my prayers!! It was a power cut!! I could leave now. I picked up my bag, and left. LEFT! LEFT THE OFFICE!!!!! And Boss did not stop me, he could not!! He had to say bye! He had to say "Bye Raj, see you tomorrow."!!!! I won! I WON!!!!!

I went straight to the CCD from office. And for those who do not know what CCD is, it's a coffee shop chain; they have outlets everywhere, in Gurgaon also where I stay. I went inside and sat down on my favourite sofa. Where I sit every day. I looked outside through the big glass window at the dark night sky; the moon looked spectacular, beautiful, spell binding. I could not help thinking about Manisha; I took out my cell phone and typed a message

'The moon!'

And sent it to her. (I know you don't know who Manisha is. But don't worry; you will get to know within a short time.)

"Your friends left quite some time back sir." It was Santosh. He worked in the coffee shop.

"Hmm. I know."

"How was your day sir?"

"Same, normal, usual."

"Have you seen *Namaste London*?"

"No. How is it?"

"Its very good sir. You will like it."

"Thanks, will catch it soon."

Santosh, my friend. The only one who understands me, and knows what I need. RELAXATION!!

Anyways, I had a little chat with Santosh. About his work, his day and stuff and left for home.

17

I reached home around 10. Had my dinner and slept. Only to wake up early next morning and run to work. This is my present life! IS THIS WHAT I SPENT MY LAST 25 YEARS STUDYING AND STRUGGLING FOR?! I really wonder at times.

But why would you care? I will tell you what happened next. What happened when after Vani left.

I meet my Juliet!!!

After Vani left, school became a drag. Every morning I would wake up and create this huge riot about not going to school. at times my head, sometimes I would be pukish. At times these tricks would work, at times they wouldn't. I had become a crybaby. Days, weeks, months and years passed. I failed to make any friends in school. No teacher liked me. Everyone found me irritating. And to top it all, I fell sick. I fell sick for two bloody long months, down with typhoid. Today if I think about it, I feel it was not all that bad. I did not have to go to school. I could watch TV and read all my favourite storybooks. I could sleep for as long as I wanted and listen to music as much as I liked. All was fine except for one thing, the feeling of being sick. The medicines. The injections. And the weakness! Uh! I lost weight. From a cute chubby kid I became a thin skeleton. And after that I never gained weight. I am, till date, a skinny boy. THE SKELETON BOY! (That is what other kids started calling me) But anyways, I was living in my dream world. I had no concern with the real one. But no dream lasts forever. Everything has to come to an end. One day the doctors declared me fit to go to school. And I was... *petrified!* I had no idea how I was gonna go through it again.

Once again the everyday – tummy – ache and fever started. Once again I started going to school. It was not nice. IT WAS HORRIBLE!! But as I just told you, nothing lasts forever. Not even one's bad days.

One day I woke up and felt that the sun was shining brightly. The flowers in the garden were blooming, and the birds singing sweetly. I did not cry not to go to school that day. It was a bit weird, but a very nice feeling. I went to school happily that day.

I can never forget that day. In class, we sang our morning prayer. Sang in chorus 'gooood moooorneeeeeeng maaadaaam, thaaaaaank

19

youuuuu maaaadaaaam." and sat down in full sync. Then it happened – enter, my very own Juliet. Rushi. She had just taken admission in my school. The gatekeeper came with her to show her the way to the class – Standard 4ᵗʰ B.

She was… well; not even on television that I had seen such a beautiful face. It seemed as if one of the dolls had escaped from my sister's secret cupboard, [which was not hidden or a secret from me by the way. (I used to invade her cupboard and fiddle with her stuff regularly)] and had come to school. She was …an angel – fair, gorgeous smiling, …gorgeous. Even her hair was perfect. Medium brown, short and curly, just the way I always liked on girls. She looked at the teacher, smiled, and said, "May I come in ma'am?" Her voice was very sweet. Even the teacher seemed to be very pleased to hear it.

"Of course dear, please come in. Look at you, you are such a darling!" you know these primary school teachers, how they talk.

"Thank you ma'am."

"How sweet my child, what is your name?"

"Rushi Sharma."

"A sweet name for a sweet girl. Children," the teacher turned around to the class "We have a new member in our class. Rushi" turning back to her she said, "we are very pleased to have you as a part of the class. I hope you have great fun here with us. But I must tell you that the session started three months back and you have quite a bit to cover up. So class", she again turned to the class and said, "Who will help Rushi to cover all the lessons she has missed?"

My hand struck up, straight, high in the air, as if I was a puppet or something, and someone had pulled the string, it was almost like an involuntary action.

"Ok, so we have a volunteer here. Raj, you will lend Rushi all the notebooks that she will need." She turned to Rushi and said, "Rushi, you can now go and sit with the boy who will help you cover the course that you have missed."

O my god! Was it true! Was I awake? Was it happening!!

Till then I used to sit alone. But that day onwards, HA HA!

"Hi!" she said. With a smile, sweeter than vanilla ice cream.

"Hi!" I said. And I have no idea what I sounded like. (May have been like a wicked witch with a crooked nose or something. I have a very long nose you know.)

I smiled the whole day after that.

And this is where it starts from, the greatest and the longest love story of my life. My love story number two.

⤜

I started liking it – going to school. We used to have fun together. We would talk, non-stop, whenever we got time. In the lunch break, in the P.T period, before class started in the morning, in between the small gaps between two periods, we would talk whenever we got time. I would tell her about my dog, my adventures on the mulberry tree in my house, my neighbours, my sister, my dad, my mom, my cousins, the TV serial I saw last night, … everything. And she would tell me stories about her cat, her mom, her dad, her brother, her neighbours, her cousins and the TV serial *she* saw last night – *everything*. We used to laugh and giggle all the time. Without any reason, we would look at each other, and just burst out laughing.

Sunshine was back in my life. I was happy in school again. I remember, once we were sitting under a tall eucalyptus tree, on the school ground. It was recess time. It was a bright sunny day, with beautiful white candyfloss clouds floating in the sky. Time must have been … like around, 10.30 a.m.

'Clouds are soo beautiful, no?' Rushi said.

'Yes.' I said, looking up with a frown and a wrinkled nose.

'See, there is a small lamb running to his mama. And there, four lambs playing there.'

'Yes'. I could see the lambs and the sheep.

She was smiling. She always used to smile. She turned her head and looked at me. 'What do you want to be when you are big?

Till then I had never thought about it, so I was like, '………'

'There must be something in your mind! Something that you want to do?!'

'………'

'How can this be, there must be something that you like, and you want to become? Someone you like, someone who you think is very great, and you want to be like him?'

'………'

'Ok, fine, but you must know what you want to become when you are big. And if you are not able to find out, ask your mom. I always ask my mom stuff when I don't know.'

'………'

'Ok, I will tell you what I want to become when I am big. I want to become a teacher, just like Monika ma'am.'

Now Monika ma'am was our class teacher, she taught us English, Hindi, general science, moral science and social studies. She was tall, had shoulder length curly hair and used to come to school mostly in sarees, pain sarees, like the ones Sree Devi wore in films (remember *kate nahi kat te ye din ye raat* from Mr. India?), and often her saree was yellow. She used to look like Madhuri Dixit a little too. She was our favourite teacher.

'I want to become a teacher. And you also should know what you want to become, its very important, my mom says.'

I went back home very confused. I didn't know what I wanted to be when I was big. I thought, I thought and I thought. And then it struck me, I had realized, yess!

I knew it. I had the answer. And I was gonna tell it to Rushi the next day.

I woke up next morning and with great excitement I went to school. A little early that day so that I had a little time to tell Rushi what I wanted to be when I was big.

I reached my seat at 7.20 a.m. She came around 7.25 a.m. We had around 5 minutes to talk.

'Hiii!' she said.

'Hi!' I said.

'Were you able to figure out what we were to do for that Moral Science homework?'

'I figured out what I want to become when I am big.'

'What?'

' I FIGURED OUT WHAT I WANT TO BECOME WHEN I AM BIG!'

"Don't shout. I got that. I am asking *what* is it that you want to be when you are big?"

'Anil Kapoor!'

'What!!'

'ANIL KAPOOOOOR!'

'Uff! Stop shouting, I got that, what I mean is that is not a career.'

I was again like, '………'

'You have to choose a career and not a person. You are soo dumb. Uff! Ok. I will explain. Choose one, you can be a doctor, a engineer, a

I.A.S officer, a teacher, a army man, or a businessman. Now choose one.'

'.........' I didn't want to be any of them.

That day I went home even more confused. I had no idea what I wanted to be, and now it was troubling me. Coz when I looked around all the men were something or the other – doctors, engineers, officers, businessmen or something. I could not find anyone who was none of these. And all the women were something as well. If nothing else, they were housewives and mothers. I really liked the idea of being a mother or a housewife. But it was sad; I knew it was not possible. I was a boy. So, I was forced to do it, I was forced to ask my mother what I should become when I grew up.

My mother is a very beautiful woman. She has long hair and all, just like Kiron Kher's.

My sister is beautiful too, she looks a little like Urmila. My dad is also very handsome, he looks a somewhat like Dev Anand. I don't know why the hell I am the only one ugly in the family. May be I am adopted! Uh! No! Must get over that! Anyway, so, I went to my mom and asked her.

"Mom, what should I be when I am big?"

"What you want to be, my dear. You should be what you want to be when you grow up."

"But I don't know."

"So search. Search till you find our your answer" she said with a smile. She generally leaves her hair loose. And always has a *duppata*, a light chiffon one, which always keeps fluttering whenever there is a little bit of a breeze. She always has the most comforting, godly smile on her face.

"But I am supposed to know it now! Rushi told me!"

My mom looked at me again, "Who is Rushi?"

"My partner in my class, in school. She also told me that if I am not able to find out then you would tell me." I said, playing with my He-Man toy.

"I am afraid that your little friend is slightly wrong there, such great questions take time to be answered."

I was getting irritated now. "NO, I WANT TO KNOW, TELL ME, *ABHI*." I shook the He-Man in my hand real hard, and one of its legs broke and rolled away on the floor. That was it – too much for me to take. I started crying. My mom kneeled down, eyes at my eye level. "Bawa, look. You must understand, nothing lasts forever in this world, nothing, not even your toys. And when something breaks, or goes away, you should not feel sad, *but feel happy, for you were lucky enough to have that thing*, that toy, to play with. Now stop crying. Come I will read you a story."

I understood what she was trying to explain to me. Nothing lasts forever, no toys, no games. Not even friends. Everything has to go away, after some time, just like Pragati and Vani. I got scared. Rushi would also go away one day.

After that evening, Rushi became a little more special for me. I would pick two flowers from my garden every morning before going to school. One for Rushi, (coz I wanted to make her smile every morning) and one for Monica ma'am (coz she was my favourite teacher, and also coz if I took a flower only for Rushi, every one would tease me.)

It was the most beautiful spring that year. Rushi and I would go to the school garden everyday in the recess after having lunch. She found flowers very beautiful, she still does. We would go to the garden and ask the gardener the name of each flower. That year we learned the names of all the flowers that were there in the garden – pansy, poppy, dog flower, shoe flower, rose, and the most beautiful and bright of them all – the gerbera.

Actually the garden was very beautiful. I really liked it, along with other gardens. When I was going home back from school I was just thinking, ...about ...gardens. Just generally thinking about gardens and walking. And then it struck me! I realized what I wanted to be when I grow up!! I wanted to become a gardener!!

I went home very happy that day!!! Ran straight to my mom, I saw her working in the kitchen, her back towards me. I almost screamed with the greatest joy, 'MOM! I REALIZED WHAT I WANT TO BECOME WHEN I GROW UP!!'

She turned around, with a smile. "And can I ask what is that?"

"I WANT TO BECOME A GARDENER!" I shouted with joy.

"Are you sure?" She asked

"YES!"

"And why do you want to become a gardener?"

'BECAUSE I LOVE GARDENS AND I WANT TO MAKE GARDENS AND WORK IN THE GARDENS!' Nodding my head after saying that.

"That's very good." She kneeled down again, eyes at my eye level. There was a huge grin on my face. "I am really happy you found your answer. But I want to tell you, a gardener does not make gardens, he only takes care of the garden." My grin started to fade, disappointed, the question remains still unanswered I thought. "But don't worry, if you want to make gardens, then you need to become an architect, a landscape architect; they are the people who make gardens, who design gardens."

I started smiling again.

And that was the day, when I chose my profession.

I become a prince and I dance as well.

In the most clichéd way I state – with time, our friendship grew stronger and deeper. I once again grew used to someone. The spring was very beautiful, the summer, very harsh. But two months of summer vacations were very pleasant coz there was NO SCHOOL! And with no school, there was no Rushi. That time I didn't mind it. Didn't even think about it. But today if I think, I wish there were no summer breaks.

That summer my family and Iwent to the mountains, in our wonderful big gray Ambassador. With huge grins plastered on our faces. Mom with her hair tied in this huge bun, my dad with that big puff, my sister in a white frilly frock with red polka dots on it, and me, the SKELETON boy, in a T-shirt with multicoloured horizontal stripes and tight shorts. We went to my mamaji's summer house in Dalhousie. It was a wonderful summer vacation, very nice. And it was even nicer going back to school after the summer vacations. For the first time I wanted the school to reopen. Although I had not completed my holiday homework, I wanted to go back to school.

That summer ended, and so did the pleasant monsoons, and the autumn. And before we knew, the winters had arrived. The year was ending. It was the time for the annual function. The teachers, for this year had decided to do the *Cinderella* as the main play for the annual function evening. And an English dance, the song – *Franky*, by *Sister Sledge*. I was selected for both the items. For one simple reason – NO OTHER BOY AGREED TO PLAY THE ROLE. And Rushi also got selected for both the items, for another simple reason – she was the perfect choice for both the roles – the innocent and beautiful Cinderella, and the sweet girl who could sing and dance on an English dance number. It was wonderful, we had to practise for one period every day, and a period was quite long – 45 minutes. I loved playing the prince –

the Prince Charming. I didn't fit in the image, but I guess the teachers didn't have a choice. And for the dance, well I know I was a good dancer as a kid. I had seen a lot of Michel. (But not in the way some children claim to have seen him recently in the past few years.) I had seen Jackson's music videos; from the day I opened my eyes. So I guess for the dance I did fit in fine. But for the play, ahum! But anyways, it was real fun, saying dialogues and dancing in those shiny, golden outfits.

Before we knew it, the grand day was here. I was soo nervous I tell you; I was sweating like a pig*. My palms were soo sweaty as if there was some bloody tap under my skin that was leaking! Apart from this, there was something even more abnormal around. Rushi was completely normal! She was soo confident and, ...composed ... that it did not even seem real.

Anyways, we performed. And both the performances were great. I don't know what happened to me but I did not feel nervous or anything on the stage. Rushi was completely natural while performing, she was smiling most naturally (may be she should have been the one trying to becoming Anil Kapoor. Well that will be Sri Devi in her case, but whatever.) And it was her smile, that made me feel comfortable and at ease. After the play ended the audience cheered like mad! They wanted to have Prince Charming and Cinderella on the stage again. We went, feeling very proud. It was really amazing, we wanted that moment to stay. But we had to rush - for the next item – the dance. The announcement was made, and I was ready, in my shiny golden outfit and the big golden hat. And so was she. In her shiny silver outfit and the big silver hat. The music started. Disco music, my favourite.

> *I was walking down the street one day,*
> *When I looked up, I saw...'*

---

* I don't really know if pigs sweat or not, what that is what they say, no?

28

I was having a complete blast dancing on the song. Shaking my head (a little more than I should have probably), shaking my butt (way more than I should have probably). But the audience loved it. My head + butt shakes, and her twisting. After the dance was over, we were again called on to the stage. The crowd went mad with cheers again. We were … stunned, flabbergasted actually, to see the response, we had gone numb. After that day, we were identified as the dancing couple. I don't know what she felt about it, but I felt great! The teachers would talk about us. Such wannabes they were. They used to say things like, 'don't you think they have a great chemistry together.' I understood none of what they said at that time. But now I know what they meant. And it feels nice.

The year ended. The session was coming to a close. There was the chance of Rushi and me getting separated. They used to shuffle the students after each class. "To open up the children" as they used to put it. But I knew for me it would work in the opposite direction. Anyways, I was aware that we might get separated. And I wasn't upset. Coz I had, by then, I guess, kind of come to terms, a little bit, with the fact – nothing lasts forever. I was not planning to spend the rest of my life with Rushi, or anything like that. She was just a very good friend, a companion, who was to walk with me for a part of my life. And who I loved very much. But I knew the fact – one day she would have to go away. If not this year, then the next year. Coz ours was only a primary school – till 5th standard.

I am followed by the hypnotized dog!

I am at a loss of words. I SERIOUSLY CAN'T EXPRESS MYSELF. I AM SOO OUTRAGED!!! IT IS SUCH A SUCKY OFFICE!! I SERIOUSLY CAN'T EXPLAIN! Its not only the boss who won't let you leave office on or before time. BUT THE DOGS AS WELL! YES! THE DOGS!! We are a very down to earth and kindhearted office. We adopted two stray puppies a few years ago. They live in our office. Sher Khan and Gabbar Singh. Sher Khan is black and white and Gabbar is beige. I went to office a little early today, at about 9, COZ I WANTED TO LEAVE EARLY! TO CATCH A MOVIE IN THE EVENING! It was Friday. *Tararumpum* had released, and it had all the fancy racing cars and a very fancy Rani Mukherji. I wanted to leave office at 6. I finished my work at 5.30. And by 6, I had made up my mind I WAS GOING, OUT OF THE OFFICE! I picked up my bag and got up to leave. It was too unreal to happen but it *was* happening. NO ONE NOTICED ME LEAVING NO ONE STOPPED ME. My office is located in a tight 'Indian urban village' kind of a place. It's a very tight and crowded place with narrow streets and way more street vendors and hawkers than the streets can contain. [If you ask me, the place really sucks and I just don't like it. While walking, one never knows when a splash of muddy water, or some other kind of black oily stinky liquid will leave you completely drenched from head to toe. Leaving you with no other option but one - BUY NEW CLOTHES FROM THAT AREA AND WEAR THEM! And just like the area, the clothes we get from there are also the same WEIRD! Available only in super bright colours. (Colours so bright that you yourself have to wear shades to protect your eyes from the glare, if you wear those clothes that is.)]

Hmm, this place! I still clearly remember the day when I had come to the office for my interview. And what an interview it was!

I had hired a taxi as I had all my college work with me and there was no way I could have carried all that in a local bus. After reaching the place, I had got down from the car frantically and tried to arrange my huge A0 and A1 size sheets in the order that I wanted to present them. With trembling hands I had put them on the dusty white bonnet of the dented Tata Indica that I had hired and tried to align them so that they could be rolled neatly into one. My determined mind forced my trembling feet to walk towards the office the nice, attractive, earthy looking building in exposed red brickwork. I walked in through the trellis made of mulberry sticks and jute rope inter twined with fragrant *Raat ki Rani*. Passing the nice and shady jackfruit tree I turned with the brick path to a bend that was a garden. And what a wonderful garden it was! Lotus pond, grapevine, pomegranate trees, star fruit trees, it was like paradise like. Somewhere to my left I saw a cave like structure with people sitting inside. I walked towards it holding the sheets tightly in my hands. The cave turned out to be a café. I was called at lunchtime. 'Hi Raj. Come sit, lunch is ready.' Boss said with a smile, sitting on a chair like a fat tomato. I walked towards the dining table where the whole staff was sitting and sat down.

The lunch continued for a good 20 minutes. He tried talking to me a lot. 'You eat very little!' But I was too nervous to continue any conversation. He told me about the office, how they all were a family and only a few days back he had rescued a flock of geese from a butcher and got them to office where they now stayed in a newly constructed pen made by 'green' materials! And how two lovely dogs had become part of the 'family', how he felt strongly about ethically correct and environmentally sensitive architecture, how free and open the atmosphere in the office was. "Everyone works the way one wants to. We don't force anyone for anything. We don't even have strict report-at-nine kind of system." Then, telling me about the projects the office was handling he said, "we are handling a huge project that is one if its kind. It's a killer! It's the redevelopment of a 10 Km long stretch of a beach in Gujrat. When the lunch was over, I was told, "You seem to be a very nice person Raj. I will be looking forward to working with you." To that I stammered, "yes sir, I have got some of my work with me, I "

"O! We don't need to look at all that, that only makes us develop preconceived ideas about a person." He said.

And this is how I had become a part of the 'picture perfect office.'

Hmm, how irritating it is to get to know that one has been deceived! Anyways, so, what was I telling you? O yes! My movie plan! Ya, so, after I had walked like some 700 m, I felt that someone was following me. I didn't look back. Went on further. I mean why should it bother me you know? It was like I don't even care or anything. Only losers follow. After five seconds, I turned round to see who it was. It was Sher Khan! I was surprised, kind of. This had never happened before. But I thought it was Sheru's habit or something and that he was used to moving around the area. So I carried on, after like another 100m I looked back. The animal looked lost. It's the way dogs look at you no? You get to know if they are feeling lost or asking for help. It was bugging! BUGGING! I was out of office, I didn't want to do anything or look at anything that had anything to do with the office. I carried on. After like another 30 m, I looked back again, the dog looked even more lost. And worse   a stray dog had started following Sheru and had started growling grrrrrrrr. Within seconds, more dogs started following Sheru and also started growling at him. He got scared; ran towards me and tried to hide behind my split-bamboo-like legs. I was stuck; I had to do something, I HAD TO PROTECT THE POOR DOG! The poor dog was asking for help. I used the obvious trick; I scared the other dogs away by pretending that I was picking up stones from the ground to throw at them. Hmm, and after that, AFTER THAT! I HAD TO GO BACK. ALL THE WAY! TO OFFICE! TO WALK *SHERU* BACK TO OFFICE!!!!! AAAAAAAAAAAAA!! I mean like this is the height of things yaar. Amazing boss. Amazing dogs! I am sure boss practises some kind of hypnotism on the dogs, to teach them ways to make people stay in office, AND TO BRING THEM BACK WHEN THEY LEAVE! By the time I reached the office, I had already missed the show I had planned for. I felt soo much like the dog in whose territory Sheru had just trespassed GRRRRRRRRRRRR! My evening plans had once again been ruined.

I put out the cigarette and open my eyes to a whole new world.

So it happened. The most feared. Shuffling. We got separated. I was put in the 'B' section. She was put in 'A'. The teachers had a very weird rule, each girl had to sit next to a boy, and each boy next to a girl. For me it didn't make any difference. The girl sitting next to me, in no possibility, could have been Rushi.

Once again I started to smile less, talk less. Unlike the girl sitting next to me. MONA! You remember Mona right? The *chhammak challo* incident? She had not changed. As talkative as ever, laughing and giggling all the time, if not with someone, then all by herself. – With no reason what so ever. [She was medium height, (compared to the rest of the class) darker complexion, big black eyes and short straight hair, cut in the simplest way.] She was someone who believed in living every moment and making the most of it (that is now if I think how she was). She was stuck with me. And I was stuck with her! But instead of sitting next to each other like lifeless, dull stones, she wanted to have fun, like puppies, or sparrows, or humming birds may be, fluttering or …jumping all the time. For like a week, I was all stern and straight faced. Answering her questions only in 'yes' or 'no'.

'Do you have a spare pencil?'

'No.'

'Did you finish the Hindi homework?'

'Yes'

'Lets play dumb Charades!'

'*NOoo*'

I would not respond to her at all. Wouldn't react to any of her jokes. But after that I gave up. It was impossible not to laugh at her jokes *yaar*. The way she used to imitate all the actresses and models and the TV advertisements. I remember, Susmita Sen became Miss Universe that year, and no day for Mona was complete if she didn't imitate and show me what Sushmita Sen's reactions were when it was declared that she had won. She would cover her mouth with her hands, shiver, tremble, and act as if she was crying (in the most artificial way I had ever seen). It was soo funny. I still can't help laughing when I recall her doing that. And so many other things she would act out, like the *Nirma Super* ad. I still remember it went something like –

'*Oho Deepika ji, aeyae aeyae. Yeh leejiae, aap ka sab saaman taiyaar.*'

'*yeh nahi, voh*' she would say and point anywhere in the air

'*lekin aap to hamesha voh mengha vala* powder…'

'*leti thi, lekin agar vohi quality, vohi safedi, vohi kaam, kum daam main milay to koi yeh kyu le, voh na le?*'

'*maan gaye Deepika ji.*'

'*Kise?*'

'*Aap ki nazar, aur Nirma super, dono ko.*'

Initially she used to enact the whole thing alone. But later I was the shopkeeper, and she was Deepika ji. This and many other ads, like the Hawkins pressure cooker ad. And many others. She was very funny.

It's true what they say; happiness comes to you when you least expect it. She would make me laugh. And Being with her opened me up a lot. I remember that day, pretty distinctly. School was over and she was waiting for her *buggy walla*. I was giving her company while she was waiting. All of a sudden, as always she wanted to enact something. A scene from *Maine Pyar Kiya* this time. The one where Bhagya Shree makes Salman put out his cigarette. "Cigarette smoking is injurious to health" *walla* scene. We were standing outside the school, near the school gate. She told me that I will be Salman and she will be Bhagya Shree.

35

I was like "are you nuts?! Every one is watching us!"

And she was like "SO?"

"What so? Everyone is watching us. What will they say?"

"Raj, they don't even know you! They don't care what you do! They are not even watching you!"

And I was like '………'

"You can't give up to have fun because of a bunch of people who you don't even know might happen to catch a glimpse of what you are doing!"

And I was… '………'

"Ok. You are still not convinced. Wait I will show you."

And then she did something, which, at that time, I thought, was completely and utterly outrageous. She turned towards the road and started shouting 'HELLOOOOOOOOOO! HIIIIIIIIIIIIII! DO YOU KNOW ME? DO YOU KNOW WHAT I AM DOING? DO YOU CARE OR ANYTHING?'

No one stopped. No one said anything. At the most, some people just turned back to look at her. And that was all. Then she came to me. With a huge grin on her face, 'see! I told you!"

And I … "……"

"Ok, now come on, we don't have much time. Ok so I am Bhagya Shree and you are Salman. Ahum Ahum. Cigarette smoking is injurious to health, *sehut ke leye haanikarak hota hai.*"

She looked at me and put her palm with the invisible ashtray forward. I pretended to put out my cigarette. Looking deep into her eyes, and said '*dosti ki hai toh nibhani toh paregi.*' And from that day onwards, I never cared about the people who did not know me. People who didn't care about what I did. People who were not worth thinking about. After that day, I never held my self back from having fun. No matter where I was.

I give my first gift of love.

That was the time when I realized I was developing some feelings for Mona. She was becoming special for me, and I wanted to do stuff for her that was special, I wanted to gift her something ...something special. Those days, international soaps were very popular. They were being introduced in Indian market. Camay had a rather attractive ad campaign. The T.V commercials were really cool, not something that we could enact, but still cool. It had all those big fireworks and really gorgeous models. Mona had told me quite a few times how desperately she wanted that soap and how her mom would never let her buy it coz their 'family soap' was Rexona and not Camay. No rewards for guessing what I gave her as my first gift of love – Camay Soap. Today it appears very funny, but that time; it was the best possible gift I could think of. When I gave it to her, Mona accepted it just like Sushmita sen, with tears in her eyes and hands on her face, "Thank you Raj!" she said, grabbing the soap and snatching it from my hand, "you shouldn't have!"

Time passed. We were all growing up, becoming even more immature (that age you know). All the other boys in the class started talking about their girls – who they liked, whom they were 'going around' with, and whom they wanted to be with. I was asked by some of the guys in the class one day, who were making some kind of boyfriend-girlfriend list, who my girl was. The first name that came to my mind was Mona's. But I didn't want to risk it. These boys were sly, I could not have trusted them under any circumstances, even God wouldn't know what they were gonna do with the list.

"So, who's your girl?" one of them asked.

I didn't say Mona. I couldn't have risked it. I said Neelhans instead. Now Neelhans was this silent, quiet, sit-in-a-corner, talk-to-no-boys kind of girl, whom no one actually knew. All that every one knew about her in the class was that she always came first. On hearing her name the boys went all "…what!! But …why?? She can't even speak."

"I know, but a girlfriend should be like her – calm, deep, mature. Still waters run deep you know." I said, resting my elbow on the table, trying to act older than my age.

They were all silent. I was successful in hiding my true feelings for Mona as well as convince them that I was more mature than them and a person of substance. As expected, the boys had plans. The next day they put up a chart on the notice board. It had red coloured hearts and the names of all the 'couples' in each. Each one had a little icon made next to it – lightning, fire, knife and other stuff. Mine and Neelhans's had a butterfly on a flower. There were, if I can recall it right, 6 'couples'. Each one had to face a lot of embarrassment from the rest of the class, for I don't know how many days. I was angry, more with myself than with the boys. It was because of me that poor innocent Neelhans was suffering. I was angry and didn't know what to do. So I pressed the panic button. MOM!

It was a very pleasant evening. My mom was watering the plants in the garden. The sun had almost set. The sky was orange-yellow. A light, cool breeze was blowing. The chirping birds were going back to their nests. As always, my mom's chiffon *duppatta* was playing with the wind. I went to her,

"Mom …why are you watering the plants?"

"So that they can get all the right nourishment they need to grow, to bloom."

"Just like we need food, right?" I said, feeling all smart and everything.

"Yes, food and thought. Right food for the body, and right thought for the mind. Right amount of light and right amount of minerals."

I was getting what she was saying. I wanted to ask her what was praying on my mind, all the more now.

"Mom. What should we do if someone feels bad coz of something we did?"

She smiled, "Very simple, you go and say you are sorry. And then try to make things right, undo your mistake."

I thought for a while. And got my answer. I was supposed to tell Neelhans that I was sorry that because of me she had to face all the embarrassment. And tell the boys that I lied to them coz if I had not taken anyone's name they would have labelled me a loser and now I was telling them all this because I didn't care what they said or thought because I knew *they* were the real losers.

Mom looked at me. She knew I had found my answers. She always knew what was going on in my mind.

"Enough of thinking Mr. Big Boy, it's time to play!" and she sprayed me with water, from head to toe, leaving me all shocked and wet and soaked and … shocked. 'Mom!'

"What? Don't you wanna have a little water fight? Mr. I-know-it-all?"

I giggled. And splash splash splash it was, all over, all around.

The first thing I did the next day – apologized to Neelhans.

"Hi."

"Hi." She looked at me all surprised.

"I am sorry."

Silence.

"It's ok, I just wish you did not lie." She said.

"I know I should not have. But I will set things right now."

"Ok."

"Ok. Sorry once again."

"Sorry, I mean …ok. Bye." She said

"Bye."

Half the task was done. But the bigger half was still left.

I went to the boys.

"Hi!" I said

"*Helloooo*!" they sang.

"I want to tell you that I lied that day. I lied about Neelhans. I took her name just like that. I took her name coz I didn't want to send you back unanswered. Disappointed!" And that is all I said. I DID NOT HAVE THE GUTS TO SAY THE REST OF THE STUFF I HAD THOUGHT. And it's good that I didn't. Because if I had, I think, I would have looked and walked differently today. According to me all was set. All had been corrected. But little did I know, what Neelhans actually meant, when she said that she wished that I hadn't lied.

The three children and their three break-ups.

If anyone wants to break-up with his / her girlfriend / boyfriend, I know exactly where they need to go. MY OFFICE!!!! Work there for three months, and BAM! A break-up guarranteed. Here is a story that tells the sad of tale three lovers, and their three lost loves.

Three trainees joined our office like some 5 months ago. J.J, Raina and Deep. All of them were going around with someone, when they joined office. They came as three happy children, but today they are super frustrated with life. And if anyone tries talking to them, they snap, like rabid dogs. This is their story.

⌒

It was 7 in the evening. The time when generally normal people are heading home. J.J's phone started to ring. It was Sujata. "Hi Janu! I just stepped out of office and was just thinking, if we could meet today at, lets say, Dilli Haat?" It was his girl friend.

"Cant say Jaan, don't know when I will be able to leave office."

"What Janu, you always say that. Can't you take some lil time out for your lil girlfriend?"

"I will try Jaan." He replied

"You always say that."

"I am helpless."

"You always say that."

"Please, try to understand." J.J really wanted to go, but he was stuck. I see a great deal of myself in him. I used to be so much like him when I joined office   all stuck and never able to take a stand.

"Understand what Jaan, that you are too scared to tell your boss that there are things in your life, other than office, that you need to take care of?" She sounded a little cross.

"Its not that I an sacred, its … " J.J tried to explain

"Then what is it?"

"Sujata, listen, it's not my *papaji's* office that I leave any time I want. You get that?" he didn't want to say what he had just said.

"Anytime? Anytime after office hours?"

"Sujata, try to understand, "

She hung up. And I don't really blame her for behaving like that. They were from the same college, had come to Delhi for their six months training. And Sujata had dreams, of having some romantic evenings with J.J, in places like Tuglaquabad Fort, and Qutub Minar, all the places where movies songs like *Agar Tum Kaho* (*Lakshya*) and *Chand Sifarish* (*Fanaa*) had been shot. In the last three months, they were able to meet just once. And then too they spent most of the time fighting as most of the meetings they planned never happened.

"Shit!" J.J said, most angry and frustrated, with his teeth clenched, frowning hard. He looked around, wanted to talk out his frustration with someone. Just then Raina's phone started ringing. "Hey Shona!" she said with a smile. They used to call each other Shona, they picked that up from *Tararumpum.*

"Hey Shona! So, what time you leaving office today?"

"If all goes well, may be in like half-an-hour."

"That sounds very good and unreal. Almost like a fantasy. Let's meet at Ansal Plaza if it happens today." her boyfriend said

"O Shona! You are soo sweet!" she said

"And you are my Blind love ice-cream, Shona!" he said

"O Shona!" she said

"O Shona!"

"Ok bye."

"Bye Shona." He said

"Bye." She said, letting out a little laugh.

Raina continued working, smiling, looking at her computer screen.

A voice from behind said, "Who were you talking to Raina?" Sitar sounds!!!!! All over the place!!!

'That was a friend, boss, a friend o mine."

"Was it a friend from office?" he asked

"No boss it wa ..."

"Was it some senior person from office?" he asked again, interrupting her.

'No boss it ...'

"You are not supposed to take personal calls in office, you know that right?" Sitar music! Going all violent!!

There was no point arguing. "Yes boss."

"So," Boss continued, "J.J, Raina and Deep, I want you three to fill up the assessment sheets of the hospital project before you leave. Its urgent, I need to work on it tonight."

"Yes boss." They all said together. It was a good 2.5 hours job, for each one of them. Deep's phone started to ring. The ring almost gave him a jolt. Boss looked at him, the look he gave was enough to kill someone. Deep grabbed his phone and ended the call. "Good then, see you all in an hour. With the work." He left. That slave tyrant! They all took a deep breath. Deep's phone rang again.

"NISHA, HAVEN'T I TOLD YOU NOT TO CALL ME WHEN I AM IN OFFICE?" Deep burst.

"Sorry. Did you get into trouble coz of my call? I am sorry." She sounded very concerned

" No I didn't, but take care in future." He said, almost scolding her.

"Will do. Sorry. What time will you be getting free from office toady?" she asked

"Are you completely incapable of understanding anything at all that I tell you! Haven't I told you, like a thousand times! I will call you when I get out of office! Now don't irritate me! Bye." He ended the call. All three of them looked at each other. They were stuck for another good two and a half to three hours in the office. All plans for the evening evaporated. These are the three young ones and their love interests. Struggling hard to save their love lives, in their own different ways.

This was like one of the many evenings that they had in the office, which, for most normal people, leads to the strangulation of love and life. One works to earn a living, and then wants to live. But it's disturbing and upsetting to see the reality   one works to earn a living, but seldom gets time to live.

⌒

That day, all the three young ones had a long chat with their loves on the phone. Let's start with Deep. That is the funniest one.

Tired as hell, Deep reached home around 11, like every normal day. He was too tired to have a proper meal so just had milk and a few biscuits. After that, he called Nisha.

" Hello, Nisha?"

"Ya." She replied dryly.

" I am sorry. But you know how my office is, right? I mean I can't attend your calls in office." He explained

"But why does your boss not understand that you also have

other things to handle?"

"I don't know, and I can't help it as well."

"But you know Deep, when the day ends, I want to talk to you, I want to discuss my *day* with you, I want to tell you what happened, I want to *know* what happened with you. I want to have a conversation with you which is beyond office and your wicked boss."

"You know something Nisha, dealing with boss in office is very difficult. And dealing with you is not being easy either. Bye." He hung up.

Raina reached home around 11.15, was very tired, had some maggi and called her Shona.

"Hey Shona!" she said

"Hey! Home?" he said

"Ya just reached. So how was your day?" she asked

"Was good, yours?"

"Same, *I had a loooong tiring day.*" Trying to imitate Preity from KANK."

"Don't you think office is getting a bit too tough Shona?"

"I know Shona, but can't really help it" she said.

"I know, I can understand. Have *soo* many things to tell you, but will tell you when we meet, this Sunday, on my birthday. Right?" he questioned her to check if she remembered.

"Right." she assured him.

"*Chalo* then, good night. You must rest now. See you sometime."

"Good night."

"Shona!" he said

"Shona!" she said

"Bye." He said

"Bye." She said

⁀

J.J reached home around the same time, quickly had the food that was in the tiffin which had been left hanging, tied to the handle of the door of his apartment and called Sujata.

"Hi Jaan! How was your day?" he asked

"It was ok, till I had that fight with you." She said, sounding upset.

"I am sorry. You know Jaan, how much I love you, but it's just that I am sooo stuck these days." J.J explained.

"It's ok Janu, I understand. But it's, my friend's birthday this Saturday, and I won't understand if you won't come there." She said.

"Yes your highness! And on Sunday, what are we doing?" J.J said, trying to sound romantic.

"Don't know, you say."

"There is a place I know, in Gurgaon, towards sector 55, on the ridge area, it is very beautiful. Let's go there, you and me, just you and me, for hours and hours and hours together. The whole day!"

"Sounds good. Lets do it." She sounded happy.

"Cool, final then, I am very tired now, I think I should sleep."

"I wanted to tell you but its ok, you are tired, so should sleep. Catch you later." She said

"What? What did you want to tell me?" J.J asked

"Nothing major, just office gossip. Later. You sleep. Good night."

"Ok but later *pakka haan?*"

"*Pakka*"

"Good night."

"Good night."

On Saturday, again they were handed work just like everyday dot at 6. J.J was most upset. He knew it was gonna be big for him this time. His phone rang. He gulped, and received the call.

"Hey Janu, I am on my way, the treat is in Mega Mall food court, will buy the gift from the Archie's Gallery on the ground floor." An excited Sujata said.

"Jaan, I don't think I will be able to come."

Silence.

"I just got work from boss. Will take at least 2 more hours." J.J told her.

"Jeetu, I think we need to talk. It's getting too much now. No matter how late it gets, I want to meet you today."

J.J gulped again. 'Ok, will give you a call when I leave office.'

Three hours after the phone call, J.J left office. He took like another forty-five minutes to reach Mega Mall. She was waiting for him. Outside. On the pavement, under the lamp post. It was dark, and late, with very few people around. She was standing, arms folded, looking at him. She was looking very beautiful, her hair waving in the air. She had come for a party, to laugh and enjoy and have fun. But her eyes were red, her kajal all smudged.

"Hi." J.J said.

47

"Hi." She said. They went inside, in silence.

That week, they were called to work on the Sunday as well. Raina told her Shona that she would have to go to office on Sunday.

And he said, " Please *yaar*! Tell your boss you can't come to office on Sunday. Please *na*!'

And she said, "Can't Shona, I am doing my training under him, he is holding all my marks. I can't."

Her Shona was not pleased. And he said, "Today it is marks, tomorrow its gonna be money."

"No Shona," Raina said "marks and money are two different things. Marks are about education, and money is about greed."

"No they are not, both give you power, both are same. They both are to satisfy greed."

None of them was accepting it, but the truth was that their relationships had gone sour. And were soon to come to a painful end.

Mona and I go to Dilli and come back in split seconds.

Anyways, lets go back to the 1990s. Where were we? O yes, Mona! I was having the most fun time in school. I still remember that social studies class in which I laughed the hardest I can remember. And that too, without any reason. There was a chapter in the history section. And we were studying some slogans, from the period of struggle for independence. *"Dilli Chalo"* the teacher said. I heard Mona making those weird sound that she used to make when she was trying to suppress her laughter.

'What?' I whispered.

She scribbled something on a piece of paper and passed it to me. It read – *kya Karen kya Karen, kahan jayeen, kahan jayee*, I know! *Dilli Chalo!! Dagad dagad dagad!!!!*

I was reading it, trying to get what she meant. Just then the school peon came and told the teacher that principal ma'am wanted to see her. And she went out.

As soon as ma'am left the class, Mona burst out loud, laughing. I was soo not getting the joke.

'What?' I asked

"O god! Look there is a frog on my hand!! What should I do??!! What what what???!!! I know!!! *Dilli chalo!!!!* Dagad dagad dagad!" she acted as if she was riding a horse. "Ok, reached Dilli! Now what to do? *Chalo haath seedha karleten hai!! Yeh kya!! Daddu* fell down!! *Chalo ghar chalen!* Dagad dagad dagad! Reached home. *Uh yeh kya!! Hath pe phir se daddu baith gaya!!* Now what should we do? *Chalo! Dilli chalo!* Dagad dagad dagad!!" she was in splits of laughter. And so was I. Not coz I understood want she was saying or anything, but coz she was laughing soo hard. Her laughter was very infectious. And we laughed, and laughed, and laughed. Without any reason.*

---

* *Daddu* means frog in Punjabi, for those who don't know.

49

Another year was coming to an end. And it was time, once again, for the annual function. And there was a bonus this time – there was going to be a Christmas celebration in the school as well. It was celebration time, and teachers were on a lookout for selecting candidates for Joseph and Mary. And guess who got selected for Joseph's role? Me!!!!! And guess who got selected for Mary's role? Guess guess? It was Rushi!! Once again we were together on stage. This time we didn't have to do much, it was just primarily sitting with a doll in front, wrapped in a white piece of cloth, so that it looked like a newborn baby, and other children dressed as fairies and shepherds had to stand all around and sway to the melody of the Christmas carols. Not to miss the big shiny golden paper star hanging over our heads. Some animals like calves and sheep and lambs etc. were also put on stage. We didn't have any dialogues, we just sat. I was kind of getting bored. So I started playing with the doll, you know, patting the doll, trying to feed the doll and stuff. Rushi was kind of taken aback, she whispered, leaning slightly towards me, without moving her lips much, with a smile plastered on her face, "what are you doing?" And I whispered back "I am getting bored."

"But I don't think we are supposed to do this."

"Why not? Parents do this to their babies all the time!" I shot back.

"Yeah, *that* is true." She admitted.

I went on, "Here, maybe you should try this as well." I made a gesture as if I was putting a spoon in her mouth. "Hmmm, this is nice." She remarked I asked her, "You wanna try feeding the baby?"

"Ok!" She was game.

So she started feeding the baby as well. After the item was over, every one who was performing with us fired us like anything. "What was that!!" and "you are sooo dead!! *Ma'am* is soo gonna kill you!" I could even hear the lambs and the sheep and the calves singing in chorus – "you are dead, you are dead you are deeeeeeeeeeead!"

Ma'am came in, "Raj and Rushi! You! You two are sooo… you were soo great on the stage!! It was soo amazing!!! Seeing Joseph and Mary doing some thing other than looking around in air! It was tremendous! The Principal Ma'am wants to see you in person!"

We looked at her, with an absolutely blank expression.

"Go go, she wants to see you right now!" we went to meet her. And we got goodies! Sweets and chocolates! It was really nice! We didn't share it with anyone; we had it all by ourselves, half-half.

Next was the great annual function! And we, the out-going batch, were to present a 'mind-blowing' performance! It would be a dance, it was decided. It would be a fun song, which would make people laugh. The song selected was – *Tu tu tu tu tu tara*, from *Bol Radha Bol*. And the main dancers were selected. Raj and.........MONA!!! She had been identified as a fun-loving, *funny girl* in school. So, I was to be the sissy Rishi Kapoor and she was to be the naughty Juhi Chawla. We were doing the first rehearsal in one of the classrooms (in front of all the children) as the audi was occupied. The 'play' button on the tape recorder was pressed, the music started, finger snapping sounds, I hope you remember the song. If you don't, PLEASE! GO WATCH THE VIDEO FIRST! AND THEN READ FURTHER!! Anyways, we were figuring out how the song was going be choreographed. I had to keep running away from Mona from one end of the stage to the other and she had to keep running after me. This was so much like the old days!! The *Chhammak Chhallo* days! We started, everyone was watching. And everyone was laughing. I was embarrassed. I stopped. I could not take it any more. My vision became misty, I could see everyone laughing; I felt that they were laughing at me. I started crying, like a baby. Everyone noticed, everyone was quiet, pin drop silence all over. All the teachers used to scream all the time in the school, threaten children, "PIN DROP SILENCE!" They would scream all the time, It would never work. But my tears worked. Anyways, that's besides the point. So, the teacher came and hugged me. Very softly she asked, "What happened? Why are you crying?"

"Every one is laughing at me." I sobbed.

"No one is laughing at you, they are laughing at your performance. You are doing it so well." I stopped crying. But what she said didn't change my decision, "I won't do this."

"It's ok if you don't want to. But do think about it. We will take it forward from here tomorrow."

There was no tomorrow. I never went for practice after that day. But yes, after that day one thing changed, it was not easy to embarrass me anymore. I remember once I spilled my water bottle on my shorts in school, every one who saw me burst out laughing. But it was ok, they were not laughing at me, they were laughing at the wet shorts, and at the incident. Not at me.

Soon after that, the session came to an end. I remember the last time I saw Mona at the farewell party; she was wearing a *lehnga- choli*. And she was looking… horrible. I remember going to her and telling her towards the end of the party, "You are looking a *Dian*."

"O really! I thought I was looking like Diana!"

"He he!! No you are not!! He he! I giggled

"He he!!" We both giggled.

"O look my dad is here! Got to go! Bye!" and that was our last good bye, our *akhri alvida*! That moment, was so much out of *Roop ki Rani Choron ka Raja*. The young Sridevi being taken away, and the young Anil Kapoor, standing there, looking at her, aware and scared of the fact that they might never meet again. The only difference here being that they did meet again when they grew up, and we didn't. O! By the way, I just discovered Mona on Orkut yesterday, like after 13 long years! I mean like how cool is that! I am gonna send her a copy of the chapters that I have written about her. I am sure she is gonna love it!!!

She was really excited to know she is a character in my book. She is in Hong Kong these days by the way.

Part 2

I have a very narrow escape from a dinosaur.

I had to change school again. My parents thought it would be a good idea to put me in an all boys' school, I would become a little tough. But I knew the real reason; dad was getting a bit worried about all my friends being girls. He never told me that, but I knew. I could never express my worries about how I would cope in an all boys' environment, I mean, they are mean! They fight! They scream, they run! *They play dangerous games*!!!!! I was shit scared, but in front of dad, I had to maintain my calm. My mom could hear my silent screams. So one day, when I was sitting on the swing in our garden, trying to come to terms with the fact that my life was completely over and things could not get worse, Mom came and sat on the other swing (we had two swings hanging from a huge branch of the mango tree we had in our garden). Her presence was so comforting, suddenly the breeze was cooler, the birds began to sing, playful butterflies appeared.

"So, big day tomorrow? New school, new environment, new friends." She said. I was eating my heart out. I was not able to utter a single word, just nodded, softly. Tears collected in my eyes. She looked straight into my eyes, and said, "Bawa, today I am going to tell you something that I want you to remember, always. No matter where you are, no matter what goes wrong, always remember, your path back home. If you fail to do something, remember the path back home. Come back home, and we will be waiting for you, we will accept you, and always support you, we will always be with you." It's impossible to express how comforting those words were at that time. She continued, "And I know my son, he is very charming, he will win the hearts of all his teachers and all his classmates." She did make me feel a little better, I dropped the idea of killing myself, and decided to go to school the next day instead. But that night, I was not able to sleep, I kept staring out of the window, it was dark, very dark, for a very long time, then there was light, very faint, difficult to figure out, then there were birds singing, the light grew brighter, and so did the song of the birds, and there it was, she had arrived – morning, a new day with her. My Mom had everything ready for me, my new books, in my new bag, my new uniform, new shoes, everything. The new *autowala* came to pick me up, and drop me to my new school.

There I was, standing at the gate of my new school, all alone, no friends with me, nothing. I was scared, a school full of nasty naughty boys, of all age and sizes, all ready to chew me up. And the wicked teachers, with witchy glasses on their noses and canes in their hands, all set to beat the shit out of me. I was put in standard VI D.

It was a huge building, with more than two corridors and more than two floors, unlike my previous school. I was struggling to find my classroom, and every one looked at me as if I was some sort of alien, something that they wanted out of their school. I heard the bell ring! I was late!! For my first day! I ran into the next classroom and by the grace of God there was a teacher there. I asked her where VI D was and she explained the way, I was about to step out of the class when I heard her speak from behind, "you look like a new admission." I turned back and, "Yes Ma'am."

"Best of luck then, Mrs. Sanjana takes VI D and she is a very tough teacher." I was scared as hell. The teacher, tried to control her laughter as she looked at me, "Go go, or you are going to be in trouble." I rushed out of the class as fast as I could, with my heavy bag on my back. I reached the door with a small black signboard hung over it – VI D. I peeped, inside, a teacher, in a saree, heavy built, tall, sitting on the table, playing with the gold chain around her neck, telling the class, "… and one thing I will not tolerate is late comers." And that was the time, when I said, "Ma'am, please may I come in?" And then, she turned, her head slowly. God! It was soo scary; she soo looked like that dinosaur from Jurassic Park with flaring nose and everything. That was it. That was the time I broke down and wanted to remember my path back home!

"Look who we have here!" she said walking towards the door, the philosoraptor! Coming towards me with those razor sharp teeth! And I could not do anything! Could not run, could not scream! "New admission?" she asked. Looking down, I nodded; she saw my teardrop fall on the floor. "It is your first day, so I am letting you go without any punishment, but remember, this, should never, happen, again." I nodded.

"Come in," she said, "What's your name?"

"Raj" I whispered. "WHAT!" she screamed, "I CAN'T HEAR YOU? SPEAK LOUDER! No one answers me in such a low voice."

"Raj" I said, a little louder.

"Go sit down Raj, and be nice in my class, or I won't be nice to you."

I went and sat down, I was sobbing by then, but no one cared.

Days went by, and then weeks. It was just not happening. I could not fit into that school, my mom was wrong, for the first time, she was wrong, I was not able to win the hearts of any of my teachers, or my classmates. I failed, so I remembered the path to my home, every day. collapsed on my bed, face down, and cried. '*Tears on my pillow.*'*

This is where it starts, the dull part of my life, in an all boys' school. No girls, no sensitive person, only wicked boys! All around!!

---

*I had turned on the song on my stereo. I know that the song didn't really spe about the situation but that's what you do in that age no? pick up the song that h the vaguest mention of what you are going through and think that the song w written just for you.

The flying Tiffin.

It was a strange school. It had an unbelievably large number of strange children, who would do the strangest of things most of the time, and most of all, in the recess. It was strange that they never ate in the recess! But did all those strange things, I felt very strange in that school, and you know what I really think is strange, the strength of the strangeness of that time and that school, that I just can't stop writing the word strange, God! It's weird, ok must stop that.

Ok. So, the teachers were… different, and I didn't fit in. I failed to make any friends, in the most miserable way possible, but could not help it! Beyond the books, the course and the syllabus, there were no common interests that I shared with anyone[1]. And more over, they wouldn't even talk to me, coz you know why, I WAS A NEW ADMISSION! None of my classmates would even look at me, except one. His name was Ritesh. Whenever the teacher was looking away, he would turn and wink at me! …I mean like how weird is that!!! Anyways, this Ritesh was unbelievably popular. He was the skating champion, a karate some-colour-belt holder and had a huge fan following. But why would he turn back and wink at me like, 50 times a day I was just not able to figure out. One day, he came to me, "Hi, I am Ritesh, Ritesh Babbar. Wanna be friends?"

And I was like, "………"

"You talk very little."

I was still "………"

"Lunch with us in the recess, we are a big group, everyone is scared of us in school."

I looked back at him, blankly, "………"

---

[1] And I must mention that books and studies were *not* really their real interests.

"Ok then, see you in the recess." He left

It had been some time in that new school and I had realized that I *did need* to start talking to my classmates, if not making friends with them. I was always told that friendship was always something deep, in which you *felt* like sharing and caring with your friends, you *liked* your friends. You loved them.

The recess bell rang, the children (if they could be called that) who had their lunch boxes ready on their benches, grabbed them and ran out of the classroom, making all kinds of sounds which reminded me of the weird tribal songs I had seen many times on TV. I slowly took out my lunch box and walked out.

Ritesh and his gang used to sit under one particular *Keekar* tree in the ground. I went there.

"Hi! So you decided to join us! Welcome!"

"Hi!" I said

"So, what have you got for lunch?" For some reason, my heart was pounding, heavy.

"I have egg omlette and parantha." I slowly opened my tiffin-box. Suddenly everyone started shouting like mad! And Ritesh snatched the tiffin-box from my hands and threw it up in the air. It must have gone some 20 feet up in the air before it came down and hit the ground. Looking at my lunch all smashed on the ground, I could not control my tears. Their screaming continued. Sobbing, I picked up my tiffin-box, gathered the food was scattered on the ground and walked away.

Tears streaming down my cheeks. I emptied the contents outside the school boundary wall so that some street dog could have it. I searched for a corner. And I cried. Harder than I had ever cried before. The bell rang again. I hurriedly wiped my tears and went and sat in the class. Before the teacher came in, Ritesh turned his head around, smiled and winked. This time his smile looked wicked, most evil. I was … outraged!

I felt like twisting his neck just like the way the possessed Revathi used to twist peoples' neck in Ram Gopal Verma's *RAAT*. But I didn't. I remembered the lesson on Gandhi Ji we were taught in 5th standard. The lesson, the teachings were very dear to me. I had to follow them. I did follow the path, I did not fight back (physically), but I was not as strong as I should have been, I didn't show them my other cheek. I decided to stay away from them, forever.

I fail.

The term was coming to an end – exams were approaching. I was not doing very well in the class tests, in that super hostile environment. But you know what? I was not doing that bad either. I used to 'just pass', used to get a 5/10, or a 4 ½ / 10. That says 45% beeing the passing marks.[1] The exam days were horrible. Going to another classroom sitting there, with a new dinosaur like teacher walking in the aisles, ready to pounce on you the minute you turn your head, for whatever reason. The teacher would exclaim 'GOT YA! You were cheating! OUT!'

After the exams, it was result time. They used to distribute our answer sheets back, in class. I would sit in the class with my fingers crossed. And that day! I can never forget that day! The G.K (General Knowledge) answer paper was being distributed. Children were getting pretty ok marks, 40/50, 35/50, 38/50, 45/50, you know, good scores. And when my name was called. "Raj." I knew I was not gonna get very great marks, G.K was never my subject. I mean who wants to know where the hell the Great Barrier Reef is! It's not in *my* house! And other things like – who is the speaker of the Parliament! I mean like *why*! Why the hell should I know that! I don't think there is any possibility that I would ever speak to him! Or help him in any way, or he would help me in any way for that matter. Anyways, the fatty dino went on, "this time we have only one failure in the class. And that is Raj." My heart sank, to the deepest point of the deepest oceans, and landed next to the sunken Titanic, next to the big blue *heart of the ocean*. That teacher, she was a pure ... !@!@$%$%^& she went on, "and he has failed because of two reasons. One, he doesn't even know where the Gateway of India is. And two, his tremendous spelling talent. He can't even spell except, every where he writes e-c-c-p-t " What a @##%^& I

That says 45% beeing the passing marks.

62

felt at that time, I had written where the Gateway of India was in my paper, in Delhi, she was such a big fat liar! "Here Raj, come and take your paper." I was taking the paper from her hands, and that is when she saw tears in my eyes. "Oooo! Look at you. You poor baby. You are crying, look children, Raj is crying, just like a girl." She went quiet for a while, then said, "If you think Raj that seeing you cry, I am not gonna punish you, you are wrong." She pulled my ear, and dragged me to the black board. '*Chalo, Murga bano.*' I had broken into a fit of sobs by then. I stood there, sobbing. '*Jaldi karo*, quick, or I will ask you to take off your shirt and clean the floor with it.'

Silence.

'Will someone get the cane from the next class. Gosh! We should have a cane, one for our own class, Ritesh, your duty to get one tomorrow.'

'Yes ma'am.' He replied, with a huge grin on his face.

'Fast Raj, I don't have time. Ok fine, Ritesh, get the cane.' He stood up. I bent down. And did what she had told me to do. The fit of sobs had grown stronger. And it was funny for the whole class, everyone was laughing, seeing me sobbing and shaking in that position. I kept on crying, but a little less harder this time.

My boss eats dead animals and challenges my beliefs and gets sick pleasure out of it.

Hmm. I used to cry quite a lot no? Anyways, let's have a little update on the office front, shall we. Raina, J.J and Deep are not in look-direct-in-the-eyes terms with boss anymore. They don't say it, but I know they blame boss for their break-ups. (They all have broken up by the way.)

It was lunchtime and we all (the whole office staff) were having lunch, together! Our lunch comes from this N.G.O next to our office that helps orphan girls to earn a little money to support themselves by providing food to people like us, who by the way are more or less like guinea pigs as those girls, are learning to cook, if you know what I mean. And like most of the other days, the quantity of the food was not enough for all of us. 'The food is less today guys.' The sitar sounds were back again. 'So we should all share and eat, and eat a little less. And you know what, it is good for health, we Indians, we have such miserable habits, we always eat more than we should.' Hearing that I was going all GGRRRRRRR inside. 'That is the reason most of us have such huge bellies.' GGRRRRRRRRRR, the sounds inside were growing louder. 'Today, we will not put more food than our plates can actually take.' And he looked at me. Anyways, I didn't care; I put as much of food in my plate as I wanted to. I knew the sitar sounds were following me, but I didn't care. We all sat down on the table, me having the most food on my plate. Boss noticed, he was sitting next to me. He picked up a piece of potato from my plate and said, 'We should eat healthy quantity of food Raj.' AND IT WAS SOOO BUGGING! I mean like who does this! WHO DOES THIS!!!!! Who tells other people to eat less and snatches food from their mouths! I mean like!!!!!! UH! But

I could not do anything! Anything at all!!! It's very very sick to be stuck up like that!

After a while, I don't really know how, the conversation shifted to non-vegetarian food. And it was very apparent from the expressions on my face that I was not really enjoying the convo. So boss asked me, 'Why Raj? You look uncomfortable?'

'Boss I am not very ok with eating animals.' I said, very straight faced.

'Is it that you never eat meat?' he said looking at me, with his head tilted on one side.

'I have meat only if it is getting wasted leftovers, I very strongly believe that food must not go waste.' I said, feeling like a man of great principles.

He chuckled, 'so you eat only leftover dead animals, only leftover meat. Huh huh huh!' he chuckled again. I was offended, but didn't show it. He looked at me closely, sensed my feelings, and went on, 'But why are you not ok with the idea of having meat?'

I was offended, beyond limits, I looked up, straight into his eyes, "I am not ok with animals being killed, cut into pieces, put in hot burning oil, dipped in gravy, and being served to eat."

Boss looked at me, his eyes all bright and shiny, he was getting cheap thrills out of it. "What nonsense, in that case, we should not be ok with plants being cut and eaten as well." He said, trying to suppress his smile. "They also can feel. I think you have got it all wrong. Every being on this planet has a reason for its life, it's existence. These animals that we eat are good for nothing else, but to be eaten. They are poultry. So it is completely fair to eat them. That is the reason for their existence, that is the role that they are here to fulfill." After saying this he stared laughing and looked around at everyone. And everyone started laughing, just because their boss was laughing. Bloody $%^*#$

But it was scary also; the way he was talking. For the last few days he had been hinting to me that I had been sitting quietly in front of my computer and doing nothing. Just pretending that I was busy working. And that time he sounded as if, God! He sounded like, if, someday, if he found me of no use for the office, he would cut me up into into pieces, dip me in gravy, and eat me. These days anyways I don't have a life beyond office; I actually felt that I had no reason for existence, no role to fulfill, beyond working in that hellhole!

I get another name — Didi!

Things were getting worse in school, I had no idea of what was to happen – I was to get a new nickname. It was one of the usual days in school during recess. I could not figure out that what the problem with that rascal Ritesh guy was, he just wouldn't stop troubling me. I had just finished my lunch. (And thank god for that! Otherwise again it would have had a Spiderman-jump in the air) "So, what did you have today for lunch? EGGBOY?" I didn't react. I just got up and I got up and started walking away. "WHERE YOU GOING EGGBOY! TO HATCH YOUR EGGS? QUACK QUACK QUACK!" I heard him shout. I don't know why I did it but I turned around and said, 'It's cock-a-do-ku, and not quack, quack, quack.' He came towards me, angry eyes, brisk steps and pushed me back. "What!" He said, and pushed me again, "Huh? What? You gonna teach me how eggboys sound huh!" he pushed me again for the third time now! God! What was wrong with him! I mean three times? I got very irritated, and pushed him back. Everyone went 'HUOOOOOOOOOOOOO' in chorus. His eyes were emitting fire, he came closer, grabbed my collar, "what do you think you are doing huh? What do you think you are doing?" I was not scared of him, and why should I be, if he did anything, I would go to the principal and tell her everything, just like I was planning tell about Dino. His hand was very close to my mouth. So, I bit him, I bit him real hard. Tiny droplets of blood appeared on his wrist. With a jerk he pulled his hand back, took a close look and gave me a punch in the gut with the announcement, "Hey people! Raj, See what he did! He tied me a rakhi! See!" He raised his arm and showed his wrist to everyone. 'From today on, we will all call him DIDI! This is what his name is from now on." He turned around and looked at me, held still for three seconds and came back and gave me another punch. I fell down. His huge crowd followed him. And that is what I was called in school, for the next 3 years – Didi.

⌐

It's not that I never tried making friends in school, I did. But they were all such dumb duds! I mean they could not think of anything beyond WWF (that is what it was called then) and videogames! Jerks they all were! No values, nothing. They would steal chalks, dusters, break chairs, uff! And God knows what not! I remember there was this boy called Amit. He looked like someone sensible. I tried talking to him once or twice. I tried telling him, Gandhi ji and his philosophy. I tried talking to him about how non-violence was such a great weapon. How we should not feel ashamed to do any kind of work, ranging from sweeping toilets to working on big things in offices, to build nations. And what a great lady Mother Teresa was, and how much I respected her. But he would never react or respond. He would just sit silently. It took me a little time to realize that he was not more sensible or anything; he just didn't talk. I was getting all lost and needed help. And no points here for guessing – who I went to – MOM!

That evening Mom was sitting in the lobby, with Anu, my sister, helping to solve her Math problems, Anu is 3 years elder to me, so that time she was studying more complex math forms. And I used to stay away when math was around. After she was through with Anu, I went to her, "Mom, I don't have any friends in school, there is no one I can talk to. I am not able to mix up with them." She looked at me, her looks made me calm. "And why may I ask is that?" she said in her soothing voice. "No one understands me, they are very immature, all they do is shout and fight and break things. They can't talk about anything that makes sense." I looked at her.

"So you have all your answers, you do know the reason for you not having any friends." She looked back at me.

"Yes. But it's troubling me. I find it very tough to deal with them."

She continued looking at me, took a deep breath and said,

"Many times, people don't get proper resources, proper guidance. Their growth becomes incomplete. Many times they realize things later than others. You should not feel bad or get upset about it. You should feel privileged, that you were lucky to get proper resources and guidance. You should not feel angry with them, you should have compassion for them and help them to grow, whenever you get a chance, whenever they need it." She smiled; it was as if she knew everything that had happened in school that day. There was a long pause after that. "YO!" she exclaimed suddenly, "so tell me, which good serial is gonna be on TV tonight!"

"*Tehkikaat!*" I exclaimed.

"And?"

"*Kashish!*"* And the two of us went to have a wonderful TV evening.

But that conversation didn't really calm me down; because what mom said meant that there was no quick solution to it. I had to stay there, in those conditions, and try to adjust, wait for those monkeys to grow, to… like shed their tails or something. And I didn't see it happening any time soon.

---

* Kashish is still one of my most favourite T.V serials of all times. Remember, the wonderful romantic comedy? Malvika Tiwari starred in it. And Kalpana Iyer was also there if I am not mistaken. (The mane of the main characters who fall in love were Rahul and Mona.!!!)

I get the best parting gift ever.

One can never predict what would happen to one in the future, and life has a way of throwing stuff onto your face when you least expect it. I remember very distinctly that cold February morning, when I was informed, that my *Nanaji* had passed away. He was ninety plus. We knew it was to happen. But you know, it's weird, even if we know that someone's end is near, we still cry. Still want him back. We still want to see him more, one last time. I remember talking to him for the last time on the phone. It was some three months before his death. I can't remember the whole conversation but what I very distinctly remember is this

"*Namaste Nana ji,* how are you?"

"*Namaste Namaste! Mai theek hoon,* how are you?"

"*Mai ek dum theek Nanaji!* Good man the *lalten!*" that is something we always used to say to each other whenever we felt very good.

"*To, kab milne aa rahe ho apne budhe nana se?*"

"Very busy with work these days *nanaji,* March *main hi aa paonga.*"

"*Haan? Kya? Beta awaz* clear *nahi aa rahi hai.*" he was a little hard of hearing.

"I will be able to come only in March *nanaji.*" I said again, a little louder this time.

"March *bahut door hai beta. Febuary ke baad mai nahi rahunga.*"

"*Nana ji! Aap bhi na!*"

And he was right! He knew it! The phone call that morning confirmed it. My mother informed me. It was his grandson's (my cousin's) birthday the previous night. He had turned 18. Mom had also gone to be a part of the celebration.

70

"But how did it happen Mom? Last time the doctors were saying that everything is normal and under control. His asthma also." It still had not hit me. Mom was sounding very composed and calm.

"That's the way God wanted him to leave my son. Peacefully. He was very happy last night. He just could not stop smiling." She said. I could sense her feeling of loss, her sadness. I could see the glowing face of my Nanaji. I was short of words. I didn't know what to say.

"Mom, you all right *na*?"

"Yes."

"I will take the next bus to Jalandhar. Will reach there around seven in the evening."

'Yes, you take the next bus and come. But his cremation will take place this afternoon. You won't be able to attend that.'

"Mom! Please postpone it by a day. I want to be present at the ceremony."

"That is how he wanted it son. That is how he wanted it. But come as soon as possible. He wants you here."

After the call my vision became misty, I started to pack my stuff. Then it struck me I had to inform someone in the office! I HAD TO CALL BOSS!!! But this time I did not hesitate. I ran through my phonebook in my cell and called him.

"Calling Boss ..."

The screen displayed.

"Hi Raj, good morning." The boss sang.

"Boss I won't be able to come to office today." I was just not able to speak.

"And why would that be?" He sang on.

"My grandfather passed away last night." I was finding it very hard to speak.

"O! I am sorry to hear that. You are a young man, and should be strong. And face such hard realities of life."

"........"

"Your family must be needing you." I was a little surprised to hear that. "I have just one line to say Raj, I want you to leave as soon as possible," I could not believe my ears! How could he be so ... "And come back as soon as possible." There you go, thank God every thing was the same, he was the same, AN ASSHOLE! "Here in India the customs tend to stretch long. As professionals we can't afford that. As a young man who is growing and has a lot to learn, you should know how to handle such situations. So I want you to leave as soon as possible, and come back as soon as possible. Ok?" he repeated.

"I got that boss." AND I HUNG UP!

Everyone at home was very calm. We all knew it would happen. But I was not ok with it. I wished I could have seen him one last time. Met him one more time, in this life. just one more time. My grandfather had been reduced to a photograph from a living person. And I was not there when he was leaving. Damn the office! Damn the ways of the world! my Mom was in a white suit, and a white *dupatta*, waving fondly in the air as if bidding farewell to some one, saying "I will always remember you. You will always live with me, in me." I could not hold back my tears. The longest stream of tears ever started flowing down my cheeks. I went and hugged my Mom. And she hugged me back, tight. "Mom." I whispered.

"Shhhh. No, don't be sad, he is watching us, this is not how he wants you to be." I hugged her even harder. Closing my eyes tighter, trying to fight back the tears. "He is still with us. He will always be with us." I pulled myself back and wiped off my tears.

We have a very large family, a very large, big-mouthed family.

After a few hours, I realized that the whole family was there. All my relatives, walking around, slow, eyes down. My mother informed me that he had every thing planned for his ceremonies. He wanted us to cremate him as soon as possible. Then he wanted the whole family to gather in his old ancestral house for 3 days and 3 nights.. E-v-e-r-y-o-n-e! Under one roof! He wanted every one to sort out all the differences with each other. After that he wanted all the young men in the family to go and organize *langar* in the villages that he had once helped set up and develop. He was a great man. Back in the early fifties, he was in a very high post in the government services.

All was done as he wanted. We all did stay in the old ancestral house he had in Gurdaspur, a small, almost a village like town in Punjab, near the Pakistan border, where no matter where, what shop you go to, people never fail to ask you, "You are new in this town. Have you come here for a job?"

It took around a week; he kept us busy, on our toes, for a week. The last *langar* was over. I came back tired, and crashed in his old rocking chair. I closed my eyes and started to rock the chair, slowly. Tears started rolling down my cheeks again. I could see his face clearly. I remembered the time when he had once fallen very ill. That time we thought he was not going to survive. I remembered sitting next to him, holding his hand. He was breathing heavily. "Raj." He said. I looked at him. "I want you to do something for me."

"Anything you say *Nanaji*, anything for you."

"I want you to be happy. Always. Can you do that? Can you take care of yourself, and be happy, always?"

I started crying again. Wiped my tears with the back of my hand, nodded my head, and said, "Yes *Nanaji*, yes."

"But you don't seem to be doing a good job at it." He said.

"I will start working on it, this moment on." I smiled with eyes full of tears, holding his hand tight.

Sitting there in that rocking chair, I wanted to do something for him. But what, I could not figure out. And then it struck me, if I wanted to do anything for him; I should try and cheer my self up. Try to make myself happy. I started packing my stuff. I decided to go to Dalhousie. My *Nanaji* had a small cottage there. We used to go there every summer, to spend time together. That was the only thing that had any potential of cheering me up at that time going to the cottage and staying there. Sitting on the bench in the garden, amidst the tall mountains, the tall deodar trees. I packed my bag and took the next bus to Dalhousie. The place was the same, as beautiful as ever. The small cottage, that always smelled of the herbs that my grandfather used to grow in the garden.

It was evening time. The sun had almost set. A small yellow electric light bulb was lit in the cottage, faintly illuminating the garden. I was sitting there, on the bench. Relaxed, a feeling that I had completely lost touch with, living in the super-fast life in Gurgaon. I was staring at nothing, air maybe, recalling all the sweet times I had spent with my Nanaji, when I noticed small-white-something floating in the air. It was snow it had started to snow. I always used to sit on that bench in the summers and ask him "why does it never snow when we come here?"

And he always used to smile and say, "It will, one day it will, you will see."

I could soo hear the background score from *Black*. I stretched my hand out. A few snowflakes settled gently on my palm. Within minutes the whole landscape turned silver. I looked up. It was the perfect parting present. "Thanks *Nanaji.*" I said. And closed my eyes.

I am told that I am a strong and sensitive man.

Sitting in the bus for eight long hours was not easy. Coming back to Gurgaon from Jalandhar felt like being thrown once again into a jar of mixer grinder and being cut by sharp, shining stainless steel blades, spinning at top speed. Ghuuuuuu! But I had to jump into it, in order to survive and earn my living. I spent my time in the bus listening to music and sleeping.

Finally, I saw the tall telecom pylons, which, for me, mark the beginning of Delhi. AND MY GOD!! THE FEELING THAT I GOT AT THAT TIME! IT WAS NOT A NICE FEELING! Once again I had to go to office! Once again I had to see my boss's face, which looked so o much like an egg, specially as he shaves his head every month. In fact most of the people in office are either bald or shave their heads. At times I have nightmares of the world being taken over by baldies, becoming one of them! It's horrible I tell you! Waking up in the middle of the night, all sweaty, throat parched!

Anyways, I had one final evening to live, and then it was over - office again. I reached home in the evening, relaxed, woke up the next morning, got ready, walked to the rickshaw stand, took a rickshaw to the auto stand, took an auto to the bus stand, boarded the overcrowded bus full of sweaty people, got off at the crossing of the "Urban Village". The weirdness of the place never failed to amaze me, you get to see the weirdest of things there cows jumping into peoples' houses, bulls eating vegetables from the street vendors' trolley, peacocks, screaming monkeys running after screaming children (and sometimes vice-versa), weird teenage boys wearing weird stuff, girls / ladies with the longest *ghoonghats* ever, so much so that you can't even make out that they have a face all kinds of stuff. It's a ten min's walk for me if I walk alone I walk very fast, I have very long legs you know. I reached office; I entered

75

the studio, "Morning Raj!" the sitar sounds!!

"Morning boss." I said, with a straight face.

"How are things at home?" he sang.

"Things ok boss, I hope the project I was handling is under control."

"You absolutely forgot about coming back, but we managed. We always manage to get people to replace someone, for a few days." He looked straight into my eyes. I knew what he was trying to hint – it was no big deal for him to chuck me out of the office or replace me.

"I couldn't really help it boss, I respect life more than work." He looked back at me, followed by a seven seconds silence.

"We will have a meeting about the project you were handling in a while, go settle down, I will see you with all the work, where you left it, in like 17 minutes?"

"Yes boss."

And so the meeting started. I went in with the drawings the plans, the sections the sheets. He started encircling areas on the plan. "We need a small produce market here, a toilet here, some kiosks here," there was a short pause, "and a *shamshan ghat* here," he looked up, 'A cremation ground.'

"Yes Boss." I replied.

"You must have visited one recently, no?"

"I did boss."

"Good! Great! We must make the full use of all the knowledge and information we gather, and since you have a first hand experience, we must use it! To the fullest! It is our foremost duty as architects to construct better living environment, for people, for ourselves. You must have noticed some shortcomings in the design of the cremation ground you went to. Let's try to give this place a better one." he said, with a smile.

"Yes boss." I said with a straight face, this time, looking at him.

"So can I expect to see the design in the next two hours?" his eyes all bright and shiny.

"Yes boss." My voice was dull and emotionless.

While all this was happening, Manisha, who was also sitting in the studio, was listening to all this. O! you don't know who Manisha is! Ok, now is the time when I tell you who Manisha is.

Manisha works with me in the office. She is one-and-a-half foot shorter then me, and five years older to me. But she looks five years younger to me, I think. She is, by far, the most pleasant person to talk to, I have ever come across (other than my mother that is). She is extremely soft spoken, always has a radiant smile on her face. In short, she is one of the very few girls, whom I actually find beautiful, from inside, as well from the outside. Whenever I have any doubts or questions to which I can't find any answers, I just walk to her, like a zombie, as if I were sleepwalking or something. I never feel uncomfortable to pour my heart out and tell her exactly how I feel. It just comes out naturally. Some people have it in them you know   the power to make you feel at ease, which makes you trust them? She is one of them. And by the way, she is a scorpio. I mean that's her sun sign.

Anyways, so I went back to my workstation, starting to design the cremation ground, struggling hard to hold my feelings inside. It was then that, I heard a soft voice from the back, "It takes great courage and strength to do what you are doing." It was Manisha, her voice, was always unmistakable. I turned around to see her. The look in her eyes was very comforting. My vision started to get a little misty. "I am putting in my best." I said struggling to smile.

"I know, I can see that." She said, walking towards me.

"I just can't stop seeing the cremation ground where my *Nana ji* was cremated. It was so difficult that morning, collecting the remains, separating the bones from the ashes." I said, my voice breaking at times.

'You know Raj, you are a very sensitive person. And you are very lucky to be this way. Not everyone can feel things as you feel, feel as deeply as you do. "It's a great strength – sensitivity". One day, it will take you places.' She came and sat on the chair next to mine.

"Thanks." I said.

"You know something; I know of a beautiful place, in Gurgaon, a place soo beautiful that it refreshes one's senses. I want to take you there, today evening. After office."

"Ok." I said.

That day during lunch boss said in front of everyone, "Raj, you are a very emotional person, you must learn to ..."

"I know boss." I interrupted him. "And I feel it's good, its my strength." he didn't argue.

I become an 'over-morning' star.

Going through all the trauma in school is, I think, the reason why I have such strong feelings against, power, alcoholics, and other such stuff. All the 'strong' MEN who go running and crying to the nearest liquor shop when ever they are in the slightest emotional turmoil. Uh! It disgusts me. Bloody 'smoking-relieves-tension' guys. Bloody 'we-are-soo-macho' guys! My foot! MY FOOT MY FOOT MY FOOTTT! I am sure it started with Ritesh in school – my hatred for people who are drunk with their physical power. Bloody the whole school used to hero worship that villain! UH!

My days of happiness in school were enduring. Very soon I reached the IX standard. Most of the monkeys were evolving. Some had actually started to shed their tails. It dragged half attached behind them. We were studying the original Shakespearian play – *The Merchant of Venice*. My English teacher, Mrs. Bajwa was more than happy to see my genuine interest in Shakespeare. I remember very distinctly when we were reading Act one scene two. The one in which Portia expresses her feelings about the suitors who had come to ask for her hand in marriage from various corners of the world. That was the time our family was looking for a match for one of my cousins. It was true then, as it is today – searching for a suitable guy is not easy. The minute you announce that you are looking for a match, all the jokers and jerks alive on the planet come running to you, grab you by the arm, and scream, loud in you face, MARRY ME! MARRY ME! MARRY ME! All of them together! Just as it was in the play - the various suitors for Portia, when she says, for County Palatine,

'He doth nothing but frown, as who should say,
"If you will not have me, choose": and hears merry tales
and smiles not.'

And for French lord Monsieur Le Bon,

> '*God made him, and let him pass for a man, in truth*
> *I know it is a sin to be a mocker:*
> *But he! He is every man in no man; if a throstle sing, he falls straight a*
> *capering:*
> *He will fence his own shadow:*'

I could not help laughing out loud in the class. Ma'am was really thrilled to see some one enjoying Shakespeare so much. The literary week was around, that time. Mrs. Bajwa strongly recommended my name for the extempore competition (god knows what she saw in me). On her recommendation, my name was put in the list of participants – she was a very senior teacher. No one even asked me if I wanted to participate or not. What she said; was always final. And saying no was like… being disrespectful. Nothing particularly interesting had happened for quite some time in my life. I mean how great it be, going to the stage, not being able to utter a single word and coming back. Just like the little Anjali in *Kuch Kuch Hota Hai*. How dramatic that would be! I didn't really have anything to lose anyways. I had already been identified as the weirdo.

Anyways, the final day came. We were all dressed in our uniforms – navy blue blazers and gray trousers – the most boring clothes on earth. All the master debaters were just chewing everyone RAW! The teachers were going around holding forth. Speaking on everything. Whether any of it made any sense or not. There was a big loud round of applause for every participant as he left the stage. My turn came. I was offered a bowl full of chits. I picked up one. It read – "*An encounter with a Somnambulist in an express train.*" It very hard to control my laughter. I didn't even know what the hell Somnambulist meant, imagine talking about an encounter with one! I told the teacher incharge. 'I don't know what it means!' with great confidence.

'The one who sleep walks. Now cook up a story. Fast.' She said. I had two minutes. I had a small outline of a story in mind before I stepped onto the stage. I looked at the audience. I saw Mrs. Bajwa sitting in the judges' panel. I passed her a smile. She smiled back. I forgot all the instructions I had been given in the past few days – DO NOT LOOK INTO ANYONE'S EYES AT ALL, LOOK ABOVE EVERYONE'S HEAD. And I started, with the normal stuff. "Good morning everyone. It's a beautiful day. Isnt it? Today I am here to tell you about my encounter with a somnambulist in an express train, which, by the way, has never happened. And I didn't even know the meaning of the word till three minutes back there, in the green room. But thanks to Mrs. Rai, now I know, it's a noun, meaning a person who sleep walks. God! My hands were sweating soo much back there before I stepped on that stage that I was thinking of getting a bucket with me." There was a roar of laughter. "Ok, about this insident never actually happening. I do have a small story, made up for you. Here it goes. Most of my cousins had come over to my place this summer vacations. And we planned to go to Delhi. You know, to see the normal stuff – Taj Mahal, Qutub Minar, Red Fort ..." there was another roar of laughter. "I know I know, Taj Mahal is not in Delhi, but the story is a piece of fiction no? So I am allowed to say so." More laughter followed. "So, we planned to go by train, at night. And I must tell you when we all get together, we all go bananas." More laughter. "No seriously." And more laughter. "So we were having fun, playing cards and all, having bananas" more laughter "when we suddenly saw a man approaching us, in the semi darkness. There was something very weird about him." I looked at Mrs. Bajwa and other judges. They had nice smiles on their faces. I was laughing through all this anyways. Just then I heard the warning bell. I just had thirty seconds to wrap up and finish my thing. "We all saw him and got scared. AAAAAAAAAA! And everyone in the train woke up!" I gave a little pause. Every one was silent. "that's it! The story is over! Thank you all very much." And I stepped off the stage. The round of applause, was, the longest and the loudest. I had done it! In front of everyone! Proved to the WHOLE SCHOOL THAT I COULD SPEAK! I stepped off the stage all sweaty and shirvering! Those mean boys, were all sitting there. I was not so sure about what I had done on the stage. *Was it right to talk like that, in such an informal way?* I didn't know. And I really didn't care! It was over. But it was fun! After me there were two more contestants. And after a five minutes filler item – a song sung by some weirdo, '*gur nalon ishq mitha*' (that's what they always sang in all the schools in punjab as filler items no?) the results were announced. I was very faintly optimistic about getting some position in the compitition. Mrs. Rai stepped on stage "I have the results here with me. Any one wants to know?" she said into the mike. "YEEAASSSSSSSSSS" the whole hall screamed. "Ok then, there it is. A special consolaton prize goes to…" I was very optimistic about this, I deserved this! yes! They had decided to give a special consolation prize this year!!! To me!!! "Vinay!" every one cheered. I didn't. I knew I had lost! Lost it to fat-as-football Vinay! He went on stage and collected the trophy, showing it to the audience, just the way one is supposed to. 'The third prize goes to… any guesses?' different boys screamed diffefernt names. "RAVI!" she screamed! The croud cheered again. UH! Stupid rabbit lookalike Ravi! Uh UH! Could he not just give up his position just for one year! I was soo… offended! Uh! That irritating good-for-everything Ravi! "And the secont prize goes to…" she continued. And again stupid boys sreamed names of other some stupid boys. But some one said my name as well, I looked at Mrs. Rai all wide eyed each and every muscle in my body (if there were any) all tensed. "RITESH!" she screamed again. This time bloody louder than the last time. Thank god her lungs didn't go out flying, hitting the opposite wall of the auditorium. Huh! That VILLAIN. I didn't know why he won. And WHY EVERYONE WORSHIPPED

HIM SO MUCH. The judges were partial! Anyways, after the second prize was announced, I lost all hopes. My shoulders drooped and I turned around. There was no point staying there anyways. "AND!" she screamed again. "THE FIRST PRIZE GOES TO...... ANY GUESSES?" I had already started to walk away. 'YES, ANY GUESSES?' and everyone screamed my name, in divine unison. 'RAAAAAAAAAAJ' I COULD NOT BELIEVE MY EARS! IT COULD NOT BE POSSIBLE! I MEAN LIKE HOW! HOW!!!! HOW!!! "YESSSS!!! RAAAAJ!!!" She screamed unbelievely loudly! I was too ... Shocked to turn around to look if her lungs had gone smashing against the wall. Loud cheers and screams followed! My shoulders dropped even more. My vision became misty, tears collecting in my eyes. Was it ... real? I was completely overwhelmed! "Come Raj, take your trophy." I nodded. And walked to the stage, once again. I didn't realise but tears were streaming down my cheeks. Tears of happiness, that was the day I understood, and experienced the tears of happiness, for the first time. I could feel an invisible spotlight following me. And I could see my self walking towards the stage, just like Huge Grant in the last scene of *Notting Hill*, walking next to Julia Roberts. I knew how hidiously ugly I was, but what was the harm in dreaming a little. Especially on a day like that. I went on the stage, took the trophy, all trembling. Mrs Rai patted me on the back. 'Very well done Raj.' She said. I smiled, looking at her, bowing a little. Tried to say thank you but could not speak. Was not able to utter a single word. Just turned around and walked off the stage.

And. That. Was. It. I became a star. Overnight (or overmorning I should say). Every one knew me as Raj – the Fun boy. No DIDI anymore!

All the teachers wanted me to participate in the remaing two events – the onstage salad making competition and the poster making competition. I was super thrilled to get the offers. I said yes. But there were only two tiny tiny problems – I had no idea how to make any knid of food using fruits or vegetables, and, and I knew zip about painting!

I see my three stars.

A cool night breeze was blowing. Manisha and I were sitting on a rock in the ridge area in the east part of Gurgaon. It was a moving sight, seeing the busy city from a distance. The lights seemed to shiver with the cold. The long, straight, boring and busy roads; overflowing with cars. The tall arrogant and shiny glass buildings all lit up. We were having hot steaming tea and fruits, which Manisha had arranged from the tea stall near the temple – the place we were sitting. The moon was a beautiful, delicate, thin, perfect crescent. It was so beautiful that you could look at it endlessly. "It's *dooj ka chand.*" She said, "This is the *chand* we see on Shiv ji's head in the images." I continued looking at the moon. There was a very comforting silence for, at least, the next two minutes.

"You realize it only when you see the city from a distance how fast you have been running. And get time to think – been running after what? And why?" Manisha said, looking thoughtfully pensively at the shimmering lights. "Most of us spend most of the years of our youth and power running blindly after things which we want but don't need." She continued. I sat there, silent. Getting over the death of a loved one is never easy. The feeling of loss never dies. It lives on forever – to surface time and again.

"Whenever I get upset or am in any kind of confusion or doubt, I always come here. Come here to think and to reflect. I always get my answers." She turned around and looked at me, smiling. "And you know what, this is a great place to come and paint. You paint right? I remember you told me that once." She said.

"Yes I do." I said.

"Great then! What do you say! This Sunday? We will both come here and make one painting each." she said

"Sounds great." I said

"Come, let's go to the temple." She stood up, waiting for me. I got up. It was a fairly large temple complex. Built on a steep contoured land - a lot of level differences, a lot of steps, lots of ramps. We went to the *Krishan ji ka mandir* first, then to the *Shiv ji ka mandir*, then we went to the *Mata ka mandir*. After that we headed towards the *Hanuman ji ka mandir*. It had a huge open court in front of it, elevated with three steps. I set foot on the second step and suddenly all the lights went out. I was shit scared. It became pitch dark. Not a single light anywhere, it seemed that the whole city had just disappeared into thin air, or sunk in a sea of darkness. The temple was actually in the middle of nowhere. And it is a very popular belief that a lot of India's most wanted criminals live on the ridge area of Gurgaon.

"WOW!" I heard her say, "look at the sky! It is soo clear! I have not seen such a clear sky for ages. We are very lucky to have come here today, at this time!" Manisha exclaimed. I was still very scared.

"What is your sun-sign?" She asked.

"Taurus" I said, all confused. Why would she ask me that, in the middle of nowhere, in the middle of such darkness! She looked up in the sky, "There!" she pointed to the sky, "you see those three stars forming a triangle. That's the Taurus."

"Where?" I looked up all over the sky, trying to locate the constellation.

"There, see." She said.

"Where? I can't see!" I said

"Ok, look, you see that bright star, now follow that line," she ran her finger across the sky lit with stars, "that star, and the star up and below it, that is the Taurus." I was able to locate the constellation.

"Okayee," I said, "I never knew that my sun sign consisted of only three stars. That is not a good rating you know." I joked. "Ok now tell me where Scorpio is." It was just then that the lights came back.

"Too bad." She smiled. "Now we won't be able to see the sky that clearly. I will show you some other time, maybe."

"Come; let's go to the *Hanuman ji's* temple. It's getting late, and really chilly." She said.

We went to the temple quickly, said our prayers, and left.

Before we left, I looked up once again to see the moon to capture its beauty in my memory, the way it was that moment, that instant. After that day, whenever I see the moon, its magnificence stimulates me, and I always remember Manisha. And never fail to send her an SMS.

Desperate girls call me up in the night and want to exchange notes with me (and nothing beyond that).

I had already bagged prizes for two out of the three events – first prize in the extempore competition and a second prize in the salad making competition. Salad making was fun. I wore a chef's hat and an apron, just like the one Shahrukh Khan wore in *Duplicate*. I felt soo much like Manu (his character in the film.) I was to prepare a salad called 'heart's delight'. Scoop out a pineapple and make a basket out of it, fill it with Russian salad and put decorative dressings around it in the shape of a heart.

It was fun preparing food on stage. I ended up saying things like – 'and then we cut this onion into… rings… which… I am not being able to cut right now.' Struggling to cut the onion 'Look! This one looks like a distorted cylinder!' showing a piece of onion I had cut to every one. I also cut my finger a little and it bled. That gave me an opportunity to demonstrate how to tie bandage on your finger all by yourself. There were loud roars of laughter most of the time. That contest was easy.

But the poster making competition. Good God! It was *not* easy. We were to prepare posters for the upcoming school 'gala fete'. Each participant was to make a poster for a stall that was to be put up in the stalls during the fete. I was given the skittles stall. Conceiving the idea for the poster was not difficult – Mickey throwing the ball and Minnie cheering with the wooden bottles scattered in the air all over. Drawing was not that tough either. But painting it, by God! I had never painted seriously before. I mean like how is someone supposed to paint! The paint is… liquid! It drips! It spreads!! … It does so many things! Like some naughty …out-of-control …three-year-old! The poster colours were not uniform; there were dark and light patches all over. I decided to put some glitter on it to hide the dreadful patches. The packet of the glitters burst open I don't know how, AND I HAD GLITTERS SCATTERED ALL OVER THE POSTER!!! AND THE PAINT WAS STILL WET!!! I didn't know what to do. I looked around. The boy sitting next to me seemed to be very happy looking at me, as if he had won a lottery or something. There was a piece of cloth lying in the corner of the room, I took that cloth and started to wipe off the glitters. AND IT WAS LIKE MAGIC!! It was not only that the glitters went off, but all the dark and light patches, they all became uniform!!!! EUREKA! EUREKA!!! I gave the finishing touches to the poster with that wet piece of cloth and BOOM – my final prize.

The story of my success and hidden talents didn't remain confined to my school alone. Soon it reached the nearby St. Joseph's Girls' school as well. The girls wanted to see this fun painter guy. My photographs were being circulated. I started dreaming that my photos were being used for more then just to look at – for worshipping, in special temples made in my name, With *aarti ki thalis* in front and *aarties* being performed in my name with songs written exclusively for me!

I remember, one night, we all – me, mom, dad, and Anu were sitting. O! By the way, I didn't tell you about my dad! He is a typically conventional dad who worked really hard all his life for his family and never expressed his love or feelings for them ever. Never told us that how much he loved us. That all he did and worked for was, us. The reason he lived for, was us – his family. He always kept a straight face, seldom smiled. Was never satisfied with my marks or grades in school. 'Anything below 80% is completely unacceptable.' He would always say. But what irritated me more than anything was that he never considered me a boy, and now, more than ever. 'What kind of a boy cuts vegetables! That too on stage!! And paints!!!' he would say.

Yes, so, coming back to the story, all of us were sitting in the room. It was about 10.30 pm. And at our place, 10:30 is considered late.

The phone rang. My dad picked it up.

"Hello" a young girl's voice.

"Yes?" my dad's heavy voice.

"Can I speak to Raj please? Uncle?"

"May I know who is on the line?"

"My name is Meghna, uncle, and who are you?"

"I am his father." My dad said, almost like Darth Vedar from *Star Wars*, in the final part, when he says – 'I am your father!' in his super heavy and deep voice.

"O! *Namaste* uncle!"

"How do you know my son?"

"I don't really know him as such. We have never met. Don't worry uncle; I just want to exchange some notes with him. Only study notes. Won't talk about anything else."

"Tell me which subject notes, I will get them delivered to you."

"O uncle! Please let me talk to him *na*! Only once."

"No I won't."

"You should be happy that your son is so popular that girls like me want to talk to him."

"No, I should be worried that my son is so popular that girls like you want to talk to him."

He put the phone down.

I paint on the hill.

We did go back to that magically beautiful place on Sunday, Early in the morning. The place looked completely different in daylight. It was mostly a rocky terrain, with few bushes and some clusters of trees. We selected our suitable spots for painting and set up our stuff under two different trees, which were a part of two different clusters of trees. There was a row of trees, which connected these two clusters. Painting always helped me to liberate. I had my colours ready, bright shades of yellow, red, blue and green. I started to run my brush and fingers all over the canvas. Generously spreading the bright colours all over. Suddenly that feeling struck me, the feeling that always strikes me at least once, whenever I paint the feeling of blankness. I had no idea where to put the next stroke. I happened to look down on the ground and saw a beautiful orange flower, I had never seen before. I picked it up and observed it closely. The beauty of the flower induced a smile. I looked up. The tree above me was full of those orange flowers. I could not hold it any longer I had to share the beauty of that flower with someone. I rushed to Manisha,

"Manisha! Look what I discovered!" Seeing the flower, she stretched her hand out. I placed it lightly on her hand. She stretched her hand out, seeing the flower. I placed it lightly on her hand.

"This is beautiful." She said, and continued to stare at the flower for like a full minute. Then she said, "you know what, I am going to click a picture of this." Pulling out her camera cell-phone out of her pocket. "I never click pictures of beautiful objects, but let this one be an exception." I looked at her all confused. "And why is that? I mean why don't you click beautiful objects?"

"Because I think it's unfair to the beauty of the object." She said.

"How?"

"Because the absolute beauty of nature can never be captured in a frame. Only a part of its beauty can be captured. It's only unfair to the beauty - disrespectful, to strip off a chunk of it and preserve the remaining. It's only memory that can capture beauty in its completeness and nothing else." She placed the flower on the ground, observed it from various angles critically and finally clicked a picture. She took a deep breath and looked around to study the landscape. The two clusters of trees and the row of trees joining them; were full of these beautiful orange flowers. We were surrounded with those flower trees, in full bloom. The feeling those flower trees generated is tough to articulate. No words can express it. All I can say is go to the ridge area of Gurgaon and see it for yourself.

I completed my painting that day in the middle of that beautiful situate. According to Manisha, my mental state could not have been expressed as well in any form, other than that painting. I called the painting "Anger."

The fight and the flowers.

It was six-twenty. I packed my stuff and started walking out of the studio, crossed boss's workstation. Before he could catch my reflection on his monitor and accuse me of 'leaving early' I stopped and said, "Boss I am leaving." He started looking at his computer screen and at me frantically, "O!" he said, "I was just going to give you some work! In future you should let me know in advance that you want to leave early, if you need to, so that I can plan accordingly." I looked at my watch and back at him. It was six-twenty then. I looked at my watch and looked back at him. Hoping that he would understand what I wanted to say. After a pause of like five seconds, I said, "Boss, we will take up the work tomorrow."

I had caught him off guard, he could not think of any way to keep me from going. "Ok," he said. "Will take up the work from here tomorrow."

"Bye boss."

"Bye Raj." He sang

I reached home around seven. Tired as hell. It was around seven-five that the phone started ringing. I received the call. Guneet started singing "Hey Chicky! Chickey Mickey! O Chickey your so o fine your so fine you blow my mind hey Mickey! Chickey-Mickey!"

"Hi Guneet." I said.

"Where are you Chickey-Mickey!?" she said giggling.

"I am at home." I replied.

"THIS EARLY?" she almost screamed.

"Ya, I make it a point now to leave office on time. Reach at 9:30 and leave at 6." I said in my super tired voice.

"Good good, I am proud of you. What are you doing *abhi?*"

"Nothing, why?" I asked

92

"Nothing really, I was coming over to your place, so thought might as well tell you." She said.

I was very tired. Wanted to say please don't come, but ended up saying "Ok, what time will you be reaching?"

"In fifteen minutes?" she said.

I forced myself to say, "Ok. Will be waiting for you."

Fifteen minutes passed. She didn't come. I called her up, fully determined to say that I was too tired and could we meet up some other time.

She received my call, "Yes Chickey?" It was getting on my nerves now, but didn't say anything. "In what time? Fifteen minutes gone already."

"In another five minutes." she said

I wanted to say I would have fallen off to sleep by then. I struggled to formulate words. " ammm"

"Ok, you keep ammming till I come, I can't keep listening to it, I am driving, bye!" she ended the call.

There was a loud banging on the door in like about seven minutes. I woke up out of my sleep and opened the door.

"SURPRISE!!!!!" Guneet and Shalini screamed. Guneet had a small box in her hands. "HAPPY BIRTHDAY!!!!"

"But my birthday is still a week-and-a-half away." I said, all confused, and surprised. They had got a black forest pastry for me.

"We know that stupid, but the preparations have to start no? There will be a party on your terrace on the 8th of May."

I smiled.

"But before that we have Aksha's birthday to plan. Its in three days." She continued

"O yes! I completely forgot! We must plan something!"

"No sweat no sweat," she said all confident. "We have planned it all. We will do two performances – *Tenu le ke mai javaga* from *Salaam-e-ishq* and Salman's *mujh se shaadi karogi*. You play the lead roles and we will be the side dancers." She said doing a little dance step. "And we have all the costumes and props ready."

"Sounds really cool. Great fun! You girls have made my day." And then I said something that I should never ever have. "Its funny. You know what, when you were calling, I was trying my level best to prevent you guys from coming. I had such a looong and tiring " as I was speaking, I noticed that a fire was smouldering in Guneet's eyes. She looked mad. She kept the pastry on my bed and left. Shalini followed her.

"GUNEET! WAIT!" I shouted and ran after them. "GUNEET!"

The girls walked out, got into the car and drove away – at full speed.

I was left standing barefoot, speechless, shocked, wide-eyed, drop-jawed, knowing exactly what do to – buy flowers.

Ok! Now this is the time for a very important lesson, for all the guys reading this, mark my words, it's the golden rule, IF ANYTHING GOES WRONG WITH YOU AND YOUR GIRL, GIVE HER FLOWERS. DON'T QUESTION, DON'T THINK, DON'T ASK ANYTHING. JUST BUY FLOWERS AND GIVE HER!

I ran back to my room, put on my sneakers, and ran, to the nearest flower shop. Bought a bouquet of yellow and orange gerberas with some baby's breath and other leaves on the side. Boarded the next bus to her locality. Within the next ten minutes I was standing on her doorstep ringing the doorbell, with flowers in my hand. WHAT A FOOL I TURNED OUT TO BE, WHAT A FOOL, WHAT A FOOL, WHAT A FOOOOOL AAAAAAAAA!

Guneet opened the door, all red eyed, blowing her nose. She looked at me and was about to shut the door when I quickly shot in my hand holding the flowers through the narrow slit between the door and the doorframe. She left the door open and walked away.

"Guneet! Wait! I am sorry! I didn't ..."

"Shut-up!" she snapped.

There was no point arguing with her. I sat down in the drawing room, holding the flowers in my hand. Looking at them, wondering what to do. She came back, snatched the flowers from my hand and started arranging them in a vase on the table.

"Guneet?" I followed her. She still wouldn't talk to me.

"Guneet you know how important you are for me. You are everything for me, here, in Gurgaon. Away from home you are my family. Everyone else out of us stay with their families   Aksha, Shalini,   everyone! But you and me... we stay away from our families, alone, and all we have is each other, no one understands me better that you Guneet, and I can't afford that you be mad at me. You are my best friend; I have spent all of my adolescence with you, and ." My voice started to break. "And I can't afford to lose you..." My legs felt weak, it was becoming too heavy for me; I sat down on the sofa. She came and stood in front of me, still for like five seconds, and then hugged me. "Its ok." She said. She was also crying. "I understand. Work and stress, I should not have been so pushy. But it was soo much fun," she giggled, wiping her tears, "calling you all those names."

"I know, even I was enjoying that. Till a certain point of time." I said

"And also there was no way that I could think of to make YOU realize that how timid, meek, weak, and submissive you had become towards your boss. Ok, now come on, your favourite movie *Devil Wears Prada* is gonna be on TV in a while. I have ordered special dinner and coke. After the movie we will sit and decide who all to invite to the parties.

I sing and dance in the street in front of my math tutor.

Everything has to come to an end one day, and my days of glory in school were no different. All my photographs which I was imagining, to be kept in the temples of my name (figuratively of course), were now all littered on the roads - lay in the potholes, to get wet, to rot, and perish. The temples were being torn down. Primarily by my math teacher, I could see him, sitting in the bulldozer, demolishing my temples, laughing his big evil laugh, with a villainous frown, Hu Hu Ha Ha Ha Ha! The second term results were out. And I had failed in math, BAD! 24/100. Yes, I was that bad. Anyways, I had freaked out and was all lost, but dad at home did not have any doubts about the next step to improve my grades – I had to take tuitions from my math teacher from school. He always claimed that if a student took tuitions from him after school, he would never fail.

So there I was, in the 3.30 to 4.30 slot. Standing in front of his house, at 3.10. Dad had forced me to go early, (so that the teacher felt that I was a very sincere student who really wanted learn more from him. Hah!) It was very upsetting. I was standing there, under that stupid tree, in that heat, missing my *SWABHIMAAN**!!!! I was soo mad that time that I can't tell you. I stood there, cursing the whole world, for giving more importance to math than *Swabhimaan*. My dad's words were echoed in my mind, "math weak *hoga to kya karoge? KUCH NAHI*." And that was exactly when I heard a girl's voice singing from behind, "*Hey Franky!*" I turned around. I COULD NOT BELIEVE MY EYES! IT WAS RUSHI!! In her school uniform, navy blue skirt, white shirt, multicoloured tie, red belt, white socks, black

---

*Swabhimaan, the TV serial? Remember? Written by Shobha De? Kitu Gidwani is such a … ammm, no other lady can match her elegance ever.

96

shoes! She was looking as pretty as ever. The same fair complexion, the same light brown hair, short curly hair, and the same beautiful face.

> *"I was walking down, the street one day,*
> *When I looked up, I saw a friend,*
> *Hey Franky, do you remember me."*

She came towards me, singing. And doing all the dance steps that we had once done together, on stage. I looked at her, she continued singing,

> *"He looked at me, and then I blushed,*
> *Coz I remembered I loved him so much,*
> *Way back when, we were friends,*
> *Going together and then he looked at me Franky."*

She remembered the whole song, and all the steps. And surprisingly, SO DID I! After one or two gestures inviting me to dance with her, I partnered her for the dance. I could not stop looking at her. I was so happy I was jumping inside. After all this time!! AFTER ALL THESE YEARS!!!!

"RAJ!!!!" She screamed "after all these years!!!! And I have heard soo much about you!!!! You can cut vegetables and you can paint!!!!" I was a little embarrassed.

"Yes, … I … do that…." I said.

"How have you been? I have soo much to ask!!! I have soo many stories to tell!!! How is the 'boys' school?!"

"Its ok…" I stammered, and that is when the ugly evil math teacher opened the door. He looked at me, and then at her, with a frown. And said, "You can come in." And went inside. I never missed math tuition after that!

That day, I went back home, and searched through my old notebooks. After a two minute search through the huge heaps, I finally found it!! The scrapbook that I had dedicated to Rushi! It was there back in my hands again. I used to write down about each and every moment I spent with her, each and every feeling I had for her. I had pasted each and every photograph I had of her. I carried the scrapbook to my study table, blew the old dust off that had settled on it through all the years, opened it, and started writing – *"After four long years, I met Rushi, again – My long lost best friend. She looks just the same…"*

I declare myself good looking.

I had started growing fond of Manisha. We started hanging out together, more. I remember we were in her car once; she was driving us to someplace. O! Yes! We were going to watch this movie!! *Music and lyrics*! It released on Valentines Day that year. I had had seen it once, but wanted to see it again, with her. She was looking really beautiful that day. She was wearing some thing yellow, a kind of oversized, baggy, hangy sweater kind of thing, poncho is what I think they call it. Yellow is, by the way, my favourite colour. I feel it's the colour of happiness. Some *Meera's bhajans* were playing in the car.

'I find Meera ji very inspiring.' She said

'Ok' I said, sitting next to her. Feeling all dumb. I had zip idea abut Meera ji.

"You know *Meera ji's* story right?" she asked.

"Aaaa no." I am a very honest person. I never lie. Unless it is work / profession related.

"There is also a movie that was made on her once.' My interest in the conversation soared!" "But I think Hema was not really able to do justice to the role." She said

"I know!" I said all excited, "I mean, her acting was soo monotonous! And I can never figure out why her dancing is considered so great either!" I expressed my feelings with the greatest of emotions.

She gave a little laugh, "Yeah." She said. And then she told me the story of Meera ji in a nutshell.

Later that day, after the discussion about Meera ji, it was my turn to talk about my favourite and inspirations. We discussed my all time favourite book - *Meghdoot* by *Kalidasa*.

"I have not read it." She told me

"YOU HAVE NOT!!" I said. I had jumped back to my super excited state again, eyes soo wide open that might as well have popped out and bounced all over the car. "Well you must!!"

"Ok" she said. Trying to control her laughter.

"You know what it is about right?" I asked.

"Ya, a little." She said.

"What 'ya, a little'!" I said. "Ok, I will tell you. It's about these two lovers. It's really beautiful! And they are separated coz the guy has been sent away by the king as a punishment for some mistake he committed. Both the guy and the girl find it very difficult to bear the pangs of separation. The guy gets talking to a cloud and asks him to deliver the message of his well being, and love, to his beloved. It's really cool!" I was feeling overwhelmed telling her that.

That day, after she dropped me, I went to the bookshop and asked for a copy of the book. They didn't have! THEY DIDN'T HAVE THE BOOK!!! Bloody fools! These days no one keeps nice classics in stock. And they looked at me as if I were an alien with antennas doing some kind of weird dance on my head when I said that I want its Hindi translation. IDIOTS! Anyways, I placed an order and they said they would get it within a week.

I got the book after a week. Packed it in a cream coloured newsprint paper, tied it with maroon coloured satin ribbon, with a tiny flower-bow at the ribbon junction. I also wrote a tiny note on the first page of the book.

> To Manisha,
>
> *One of the most pleasant people,*
> *I have ever come across.*
>
> - Raj.

Next day, after reaching office, I straight went to Manisha's workstation. Placed the present flat on the table, at an angle of 15^0 with the horizontal, went to my workstation and settled down to work. After like ten minutes I saw Manisha's reflection on my computer screen. "Raaahul." She said from behind. "I found something on my table today."

"Yes." I said, turning my chair around "did you open it?"

"Thanks Raj, thank you soo much. I read the first few lines. It seems magnificent and ... poetic."

"Wait till you finish it."

"Raj," she looked at me direct in the eye, "you shouldn't have."

With an even firmer look, I said, "I wanted to."

We both knew Boss could come any minute. She went back to her workstation. And as she was going, she turned round and said, 'By the way, you are looking very nice today." and she walked out.

I was wearing a blue *kurta* that I had bought a few days back from *Fab India*. And everyone kept complimenting me that day.

Manisha and I had started having lunch together. There was a very beautiful bottlebrush tree outside the office café, which had a nice raw, undressed stone seating under it. We used to sit there and have our experimental NGO lunch.

She complimented me again on the way I was looking that day. "*Vasay to,* with Gods grace, anything you wear suits you. But today you are looking really good in this blue *kurta*"

"Really?! I mean like today a lot of people are telling me that. I think I was just plain lucky to get my hands on this magical *kurta* , but about the 'anything looks good an you' part, I don't really think so."

She put her spoon on her plate. "And why is that so?"

"What is there to tell about it? Its right out there! All soo visible! I am this thin ugly, stick figure guy. The snake like figure, the snake-figure-man, the worst physique ever!"

"I don't really go by looks Raj, but if I tell you that I don't think so, then?"

"... ..."

"I think you are really good looking Raj." She said

"Heh heh heh! Okaey!" I said putting some more potatoes onto my plate.

"No, seriously!" she continued, "See, you are tall, fair, sharp features, innocent looking. I mean like what is wrong?"

I wanted to say, really, ok let's look at this, chest 32.5", waist - 28", biceps 10". What do you have to say about that? And you know what! I did end up saying all that!

"Ok, and what about my 32.5" chest, 28" waist and 10" biceps?"

"Really, it does not seem to be so." She said, with a tiny frown, putting the spoon full of potatoes in her mouth.

⌒

In the evening I was having a discussion with Shweta about the targets for the day. I was talking to her all seriously and everything – all focused. Manisha was sitting next to us, and somewhere in the middle of the conversation; I noticed she was observing me very carefully. After the conversation ended, she told me, "you know, I finally figured out who you were looking like today."

"And?" I was curious.

"Amitabh Bacchan From *Chupke Chupke*, the English professor."

"........."

"Actually also a little like Akshay Kumar, but more like Amitabh."

"Ahum!" I was completely speechless.

"No seriously, why do you think you are soo *not* good looking?" he wouldn't let me go.

"Well, actually I have this complex, because of..." I stammered.

She was listening with complete attention.

"I will tell you some other day, don't want to spoil my mood oday."

She could see I was getting hassled. She didn't ask more.

"I think it's time", she said, "to get over the complex."

That day I went back with a new confidence. I went home and I tood in front the bathroom mirror. Looking at myself. Smiling. I ad come out of it the complex. I did not think the guy in the iirror was ugly. In fact I felt, he was pretty good looking. That day, went to sleep with a smile.

lanisha and I were sitting under the tree and having our lunch.

"Thank you Manisha, I actually got rid of my complex." I said.

"Why thank me? What did I do?" she said.

"You helped me see the mirror." I said.

"But you are the one who saw it, made the effort." She said.

"Could not have seen it without your push."

My eyes met hers. The attraction was strong. It was tough to old back. But I could not make the move. No. I couldn't. I respected er way too much to do what I was thinking of. Suddenly I felt like had committed a crime. I felt guilty for what I had just felt. The eeling had come and gone. But the guilt stayed. Suddenly the wind arted to feel like sharp razor blades, cutting every exposed part my body. I woke up with a jerk! I was breathing heavy, thirsty.

The quilt felt unrealistically heavy. I fumbled in the dark for water. Had a few sips. After that dream I was clear about one thing for sure! I was in love with her. Yes, I was in love with Manisha. But, in a very different way. In the most different way ever, in fact.

I share pakoras and mint chutney with Rushi.

Everyday, we would reach the math tuition a little early and sit under the half-dead *jarul* tree and chat for long hours. She would tell me about the friends and the bitches she came across in her school, and I told her about the rascals I came across in my school.

One day, standing under that tree we and were just... talking. The sun was bright and the sky was clear, no sign of any clouds. There was hardly any wind blowing.

"I read Osho magazines regularly." She said one day.

I was not very pleased to hear that. I had heard a little about Osho, I had heard that they were a set of people who believed in having sex when ever and with who ever they felt like. One of the major philosophies that I could get my hands – on was, 'one's heart is like a horse. Let it run. Let it run in the fields. Let it do whatever it wants to. When it has done all it wants, it will be fulfilled. And would be ready to gain higher levels.' It kind of did make sense. But knowing the world the way it is, people will just take that opportunity to have free sex and just... find new ways to have sex after that.

"One must let oneself free and do whatever one feels like. That is the only way to attain higher levels of consciousness." She continued.

I did not really understand what she was saying. So I kept quiet. We didn't notice it happening but the winds turned very strong. It was a storm. We could also see thick dark gray clouds swelling at a distance. The cool winds and the approaching clouds. A breathtaking sight it was. I wanted to keep looking at the clouds. I turned around and looked at Rushi. She had closed her eyes and had a big smile on her face. After two minutes, she opened them and found me staring at her.

"Why would you close your eyes when you have objects of such

…divine …splendour in front of you?" I asked.

"I captured the image of the clouds in my mind and felt the wind to the fullest. I could not have felt the wind the way I just did with all my senses active." She said. I kept looking at her, trying to figure out if I could also do what she just said.

"You know what! Mom gave me some *pakoras* today, along with the lunch. Wanna have some?" she asked

As a rule, I never say no to food, as long as it's edible, and as long as I am not feeling sick. I nodded with the greatest enthusiasm. Hmmm, the *pakoras*, the clouds, the green mint *chuttni* and the cool wind, hmmmm.

Then, it started to rain. And me and the *pakoras* had to part, the tiffin had to go inside the bag. I took as many *pakoras* as I could get my hands on, and gave her tiffin box back.

"I would have loved to get wet in the rain," she said, taking her umbrella out, "but I can't afford to get this uniform wet. Why the hell do we have to wear clothes in summers."

I didn't agree to that either. I was just about to put my view on the idea forward when the winds started to blow even stronger. She was trying to open her umbrella at that time and turned inside out. You know how it happens right? If you hold it up, over your head, it's like a big bowl, with a stick coming down to your hand. I, acting all like a filmy hero, asked her to give me the umbrella and tried fixing it. I kept struggling with it for like some 1.5 minutes. She interrupted, "Raj, leave it. It's ok."

"No." I protested, "I know how to fix it."

'Raj, it's ok, leave it.' She repeated.

The wind blew even more strongly, and I lost my grip on the handle of the umbrella. Away it went. Roll, roll, fly, roll. I ran after the umbrella, which seemed to have developed feet and wings both, like a hen and was running away from me as if I were some farm-boy or something. I came back with the broken, deformed, crooked umbrella. Holding it upright, over my head, with a few of the spokes turned up, and a few turned down. She started laughing when I came and stood in front of her. I could not control myself either. We both kept laughing. In the rain, in the beautiful weather, we laughed, and laughed, and laughed. That was exactly my idea of living, with a partner. Having fun, not worrying about the broken umbrella - not caring about the world. Just having fun, and enjoying life.

I dance wearing a body hugging red vest.

IT'S PARTY TIME!!!! Aksha's birthday today, but things didn't really go as planned. We managed to have a nice party for her and everything but … ok, I'll tell you in detail. Guneet, Shalini and I reached Aksha's place at around seven. Aksha generally comes back from office around eight. So we had one-hour to do all the decorations and everything. All was going fine. We had invited some 10 other guests, they were expected to reach by 7:30. Guneet was kind of the manager for the event.

"WHERE THE HELL IS THE CAKE! WHY ON EARTH IS IT NOT HERE ON THE TABLE! PUT THE CANDLES RIGHT ON THE CAKE YOU IS IT THAT TOUGH TO HANG A STREAMER FROM THE TUBE-LIGHT?! WHY CAN'T PEOPLE EVER DO THINGS RIGHT!" she was jumping all over the place.

The costumes were ready – long *lehangas* and short *cholis* for Guneet and Shalini, who were to dance in the background, and a heavy *achkan*, *sehra* and a dummy horse for me. The C.D with the songs *tenu le ke mai javan ga* and *mujh se shaadi karogi* was ready.

The decorations were done by 7:50. Dot 8 O'clock, Aksha entered the house. We had switched off all the lights. She opened the door and turned on the lights, 'SURPRISE!!!' we all screamed. She was expecting all this. But still she managed to pull a pretty realistic O-MY-GOD-I-AM-SOO-SURPRISED look on her face. We cut the cake, burst balloons, threw streamers, glitters and tinsel in the air, snow-sprayed, clapped and got ready for the performance. The song started the bells ringing, the mantras being read by the priest, *tai tai tai tai tai tai taiiiin, tai tai tai tai tai taiiiin , heya!* Guneet and Shalini sang along in chorous, *'heeriyae sehra bandh ke mai to aya re'* I sang along, *heya...* The song went on. I rode the fake horse, dancing, in the background Guneet and Shalini were doing all those provocative thrusts in their *ghagra cholis* and Guneet she was performing the steps a little more passionately than required. But every one seemed to be enjoying himself or herself, so it was ok. Everyone was laughing by the end of it. Then the song changed. We ripped off our clothes to reveal the shorter clothes we were wearing underneath tight tube tops and thin mini skirts was the costume for the girls, and a very tight body hugging red vest and a pair of pretty tight blue shorts for me.

Dadish tai tai dadish mujh se shaadi karo gi? Tang tang tang tang tararung, mujh se shaadhi karoho ge? Somewhere in the middle of the song I almost lost my balance and landed on one knee right in front of Aksha, I happened to look straight at her, *Dadish tai tai dadish mujh se shaadi karo gi?* The song went on, I got up and went back to my position and continued.

Both the performances went great. Every one was happy, including us. But it was very tiring, I mean like two full songs in a row!!!!! WOOO! I was feeling really thirsty. I went to the kitchen to have some water. The super hot summer the heat, the humidity, and on top of that, such heavy dress! I was soo tired and thirsty and exhausted. I poured cold water in a glass, oh! How nice it felt, the sight of that crystal clear, refreshing, fresh, plain water! It was soo nice, as the water went down my throat. Ooooh! I turned around and AAAAAAAAAAAAA!!!!!! SOME ONE WAS STANDING RIGHT BEHIND ME!

'He he,' she giggled, it was Aksha.

"O! Aksha! You scared me!"

She. didn't listen to what I was saying and said 'YES!' giggling again, 'yes', she repeated, then she covered her face with her hands, giggled again and ran away. Just like Juhi Chawla from *Raju ban gaya gentleman.*

I stood there, dazed.

And silent, for some good 30 seconds I think. And then it struck me what she meant!!!! SHE TOOK THE PERFORMANCES AS A PROPOSAL!!!! SHE THOUGHT I HAD PROPOSED TO HER!!!!!

She kept smiling throughout the party. Dancing very softly to songs like "*when you taught me how to dance*"* . Smiling and lost in dreams. With unseeing eyes, lost. It was a little painful seeing her like that. I decided not to talk to her that day. I would talk to her some other day, some other time.

_____
* O.S.T Miss Potter

I talk about sex with Rushi.

Those days were nice. Sitting under that magical tree and saying things that flew out of our mouth magically, which we were not supposed to talk about to each other. "You know what! That girl I told you about, Aditi?" Rushi said with a questioning frown.

"Yes." I said, chewing on a blade of grass I had plucked from the patch of grass under the tree.

"She went to meet her boyfriend again yesterday and lied to her parents."

"That is bad. I don't know how people can do such things. I mean don't they have any kind of fear that what would happen if their parents got to know. Or, if their parents are telling them not to, must be for a reason. Or, ..." I expressed my views

"I know!" She exclaimed. "And moreover, God! I don't even feel good saying this, but this time they actually got ...physical!!"

"WHAT!" I almost screamed.

'Don't scream!' She said, a little angrily.

"Ok, ok!" I tried to calm my self "But... how? I mean like...?" I didn't have words! Such stuff was completely unacceptable.

"I know!" She said in utter revulsion.

"What is with such people, remember I told you about the fat guy, who says that girls find the smell of male sweat sexually attractive? He had a picture of another girl without any clothes on today again. It seemed to be cut out of a newspaper, the paper quality felt like that. I don't know where he gets such pictures from." (Actually I still wonder where he used to get those pictures from!)

"Yuk! O God! And believe me! The sweat thing! That is *not* true! It can only make a girl puke, nothing beyond that. Akheueaaa!!!"

"And he and this other guy who goes to the gym and has these muscles and all, keep going to the bathroom together. It's not nice you know. I mean like what would they do in there together! As if we don't know!" I said. ~~We both had been taught the human reproductive system in school and knew how the male reproductive system worked. I mean she also knew that.~~ *

"Uff! Sick people I tell you!" she said

"Ya." I agreed, "anyways, so, have you decided what subjects you gonna take after 10th?"

"Not sure yet, but might take social sciences. Or may be Psychology, don't know for sure yet." She said, "What about you?"

I smiled and looked at her, she was the one because of whom I had realized what I wanted to be.

"Physics, Chemistry, Math and engineering drawing, these are the subjects required if you want to take up Architecture." She smiled back.

"You still want to become a teacher is it?" I asked. I soo wanted her to say 'no'. I soo wanted to her to say, 'I also want to be an architect, and will join the same college as you!' I soo wanted her to say that!

"Yes." She said. "And I think I want to become a history teacher."

"Good, that is. I don't know how I am gonna cope up with math in 11th and 12th, I have only been passing once in a blue moon!"

"I am sure you will do it." She said, as if she had full faith in me, way more than I had in myself.

"I don't know, right now I am more worried about my board exams. Which are gonna be! SHIT! HERE IN ANOTHER 3 MONTHS!!!" I said realizing that the exam time was closer than I thought. "I AM SOO GONNA FAIL!!!" I freak out.

"No Raj you won't, believe me…" that was then when the alien-mutant-head opened the door and sucked us inside the house.

---

* no no, I should not be saying all this. Its getting a little explicit no?

Things settle down.

The moon was a sharp crescent, with an exceptionally bright Jupiter next to it. Something, that one may call perfection. Sitting at my favourite table in the CCD café, I was looking at the moon. I messaged Manisha. I got the delivery report and a new message almost at the same instant. It was Manisha, saying the same "the moon." It's funny at times how you and some one else can think about each other at the same time.

Aksha entered the coffee shop, talking on the phone, as always. Seeing her I was sucked back into the same state of suffocating anxiety that I had been trapped in for the past I don't know how many days. She was one of my best friends, what had happened that day in the party had the potential of changing our lives forever. We may spend the rest of our lives together, or might never be comfortable with each other again. I needed time to figure out how to handle the situation, but it was absolutely clear that there was no chance that I was gonna get any, as Aksha had insisted on meeting and making things clear.

She came and sat next to me. I was reading the newspaper. After approximately four minutes, her coffee arrived. Santosh gave a smile as he placed the cup on the table. I smiled back. She picked the cup up and took a sip, a coffee as bitter as the moment – black, without sugar. We kept sitting there in silence, for approximately six minutes.

"Good god! How weird! They discovered an airplane in the middle of a jungle in Gurgaon! Somewhere near the national highway! My god! They even have a google earth image! It is a 1970's plane and ..." I was trying my level best to make the situation as casual and comfortable as possible but it was not working.

"Raj, you talking like this can neither change, nor improve the situation." Aksha interrupted me with a straight face.

I folded the newspaper and placed it on the table. Sat up straight on the sofa and looked at her.

"I am sorry."

"For what." She demanded

"For everything, I am sorry I hurt you." I said

"How?" she demanded.

" I should have been more careful in selecting the song." And understanding, that you had some feeling for me. I wanted to say. But I couldn't.

"Is that all?" she said very softly.

'Aksha, ' I stammered

"It's ok Raj, you don't have to be hesitant to reject me." She said, with tears in her eyes. It was too much. We had been friends since college! I could not see her like this. I could not lose the 5 year old friendship to something as stupid as this!

"Aksha! Look at me. You have been a very good friend of mine, one of my best friends, for such a long time. Your presence is very precious to me. But I don't feel like that about you. You are like a younger sister to me, who keeps getting into trouble all the time and I keep getting her out of trouble. I am sorry if I have hurt you. I never ever intended to do that. Not even in my dreams! I just wanted to give you a fun filled birthday! I didn't see this coming. I am sorry. I really am!" I picked up the flowers I had been hiding all this time under my seat, and held it out for her, "I am sorry." I repeated myself.

She looked at the flowers, and smiled. "Its ok." She said. And I heaved a sigh of relief. "So, I can expect you on my terrace on my b'day?" I asked

114

"Yes" she said. Thank god. THANK GOD!!!

"So, we are cool?" I asked pressing my chin against my chest, with a baby like expression on my face.

She smiled, "yes"

"Cool" I said, "So, have you seen any new movie?"

"Want to see *Jhoom Barabar Jhoom*, but have not been getting time."

"What nonsense, what are your plans for this evening?"

"No major plans, will be going home and having dinner and I guess will go to sleep." She said

"Wrong! You have some great plans for the evening. You are going for a movie this evening, and then having dinner at *the Chowk*, and *then* you are going home." This is what I don't like; we all keep cribbing, "O! My life sucks, O! I don't get time to enjoy and have fun", but the truth is we don't really want to have fun, coz if we did, we would!

'So,' I said

'So?' she asked

'So, we are getting late for the show. Hurry up!' I said

'Okaey, okkaey!' we both gathered our stuff and rushed to the ticket counter.

I tell you about the other jerks in my office.

Is every office this sick! Is every office as sick as mine? I really hope not! My office is getting worse day by day. Now see what happened today. G2three2 our confused, lovable, spineless, gutless surdy, whose real name is too long and confusing to remember, is handling a project, which is a killer again. It demands more work than humans can do. The office should hire more staff but the boss believes in making money more than the well being of his employees. The team consists of G2three2 and my three little children. (Poor children, office has become even worse for them, boss got to know about their break-ups and now he does not let them leave office anytime before 10 O'clock. 'Now what do you need to go home for?' he keeps asking them.) It's not fair what boss is doing. He is getting cheap labour from the children   4th year trainees, who have no idea how an office works, how a project is to be handled, have been given such huge responsibilities. They are made to go on sites, far away sites and then come back and report. Its not humanly possible, to see the site, which is generally a building that has crumbled with time, has toilets that can make any non-blind person puke (even blind people actually, with the smell), and the children, they would go to the site, go through the torture, in the super hot Delhi summer heat, and come back and report in the office. I really feel bad for them, I really do. But they are also stuck. They can't say or do anything about it. After all they need their grades and their certificates.

Today, during the first half, the children had covered two sites and reached office just in time for the lunch. They looked really tired and wilt. So after lunch, I asked them, "Do you want to go to the shop around the corner to have chocolates? If you have time that is." the weather was turning nice and I thought it would

116

be nice to go on a five-minute stroll after lunch. I wanted the children to have a well-deserved break.

"Yes. Lets go." They said.

So we all went, had chocolates, some potato chips and a coke mobile. And came back. When we entered the studio, every one was staring at us, as if we were some escaped criminals, with dead people's heads in our hands or something! They were all staring, most of all, at me, most of all, G2three2. That time no one said anything, we all went to our respective workstations and started working. It was only during the tea break in the evening that G2three2 came up to me and said, "You are spoiling the kids. You don't let them work." I didn't want to get involved in an argument, so I said, "tea in such nice weather! Isn't it lovely!" he didn't go back to what he was saying. I felt relaxed. After another five minutes, he said "Raj, you never took *me* out to get me chocolates!"

UFF!! G2THREE2!!! GET OFF ME!! I didn't say anything. Then the sitar started playing in the background. It was the baldy boss! "Hi! Raj, hi G3", he said in his normal singing tone. "Hi boss" we both said.

Then he did it, G2three2, that rascal! "Boss do you know, Raj is the new hot boy in office; he does not let the kids work. He takes the young trainees out for walks and keeps talking to all the girls in office offering them chocolates. And they all seem to like him. A lot." He turned around to look at me, as he said the last words of his dialogue. And then he continued "but he never offers me any."

G2three2!!!! $%^&(*)&)(_)**(^%$%&*^!!!!! That dog!!!! ##%^&&^*%!!!! THAT DOG!!!!

"Is it true Raj, I can see you are a very charming young man!" Boss said

I smiled, there was no point arguing. "Boss, I got to leave; Shweta must be waiting for me. She was to hand me some work." And I left!!!

'Ha ha ha ha!' I could hear him laugh as I was walking away.

I mean like what was that!!!!! What was that all about!!! How can someone accuse someone for not letting someone work!!! Is it like I was holding their hands and narrate love poems to them and prohibit them from working?! I mean like ... come on! Or is it like I go to other girls' workstations and sit with them and ask them in a very sleazy manner for coffee, saying things like 'Hi! How are you? Wanna have a cup of coffee with me, or may be ... something more ?'

God!! This is really too outrageous! He said I keep offering all the girls chocolates!! I mean like hello! I just asked them if they wanted to go to have chocolates, that too, if they had some time. It was their very own decision to go with me. They went with me of their own free will. And it's not my fault if they like me more than they like him! No, how can he accuse me for all that happened??!! It was not like that I dragged them to the shop, crying and weeping and shouting and kicking. Or shoved the chocolates in their mouths while they were yelling and shouting "NO! NO WE DON'T WANT TO EAT! WE DON'T WANT!!' Uff!!

My 10ᵗʰ standard results are declared.

THE BOARD EXAMS!!! For most people it's a nightmare! At least for me it was. I had almost flunked in my math pre-boards! Other subjects were fine, English, History, Science, Geography, Hindi. But Maths!!! No no no no no!!!!!! AND THE MATH BOARD EXAM WAS HERE!!!! It was the month of March. And I had been sitting in my room for two days straight! Trying to memorize the unmemorizable math formulae. I was the kind of student who wouldn't even remember $(a^2 + b^2)$ or … $(a + b)^2$. Shivers of fear still run down my spine when I try to remember these formulae. It had been raining for the last two days and it had become very cold. I felt that maybe God was trying to give me a hint that the rest of my life was gonna be like this, trapped in a prison, in some deep cold corner of the world, buried under snow or something! It was almost midday and I had not eaten anything. Someone opened the door and came in. I didn't turn around to see who it was. I felt a very light hand on my shoulder.

"*Mom*! Please don't disturb!" I said, almost irritated.

"Have something to eat. How will you remember all these formulae if you don't eat?" she said

I took a deep breath. "Mom! I can't do it! I am gonna fail! …I am very scared."

Mom smiled, "Did you fail in the pre-boards?"

"No, but that was…" I tried to explain.

"Son, you have to do your part. You can only put in your best effort and nothing beyond that. You should take care of only one thing, that you give it your best shot, not regret later that you could have worked harder and got better results. Rest all is up to Him." She pointed upwards. "But one cannot study when fear has taken over your senses." She continued, "Have this ice-cream, its nice and cool, it will help to distract you. The cool will help you calm down." She offered me the ice cream. I had it, and it did the magic. It was cold, chilling actually, and sweet, it distracted me completely, O! It's melting! O! It's too cold! O... After that I went back to studying. I studied all day.

The trick still works, you should also try it – When very depressed, have an ice cream.

$$\approx$$

The results were gonna be out in a month - On the net. It was 15th of April I was living a life of fantasy, a dream life, get up late in the morning, have a late breakfast, read any book of my choice, or watch a movie, watch the *F.R.I.E.N.D.S* reruns as many times as I wished to. *Grounded For Life, Dharma and Greg, That 70's Show, Every body Loves Raymond*, I didn't leave a single one! In that one month, I read every book that Ecich Segal and Robin Cook had written. I had memorized each and every little dialogue Phoebe's lips had ever spoken on the television. I didn't even bother to think what life was gonna be after this dream month ended.

That morning my mom woke me up, "Raj, there's a call for you."

"Who is it?" I asked, rubbing my sleepy eyes

"I think its Rushi."

I shot out of my bed and ran to the telephone pulling on a T-shirt. My mom couldn't help smiling seeing my behaviour.

"Hello"

"Hi" it *was* Rushi.

"Hi! How come so early in the morning?"

"I think the results are out Raj."

'WHAT?' I almost shouted.

"Ya, a friend of mine called. She had seen her result. I think we must go and check out in a cyber café."

"WHAT?" I shouted again.

"RAJ! Stop freaking out! Its ok! We will both pass. Now just get out of your bed and… take out your Jumbo Jet Kinetic and come." She said

"Ok, ok" I took a deep breath.

In less then five minutes I was in the market, in front of the cyber café. She was waiting there. We went inside, my heart pounding like anything. Was I gonna pass? Was I gonna fail? What was my future gonna be like? We sat down and opened the website.

BOARD EXAMS – click

RESULTS – click

10th STANDARD click

ROLL NUMBER I put in mine first (well! She forced me to!! Ok, fine, I was always a little self-centered.)

I HAD SCORED A GOOD 80.1%!!!! I DID IT!!! AND I HAD GOT A GOOD 66 MARKS IN MATHS!!!! (Now I could go home and tell my dad – Dad! *Ab mai sab kuch kar sakta hoon*, I got more that 80%!!!)

And Rushi had got a good 85.9 %! Above 70 in every subject!! We both were … well ecstatic! Jumping with joy! And screaming and shrieking! Remember *That Thing You Do*? When their song was aired for the first time on the radio? We were exactly like that! It took us some good ten minutes to get back to normal. After that we came back to our senses, calmed down, and congratulated each other.

"So." I said

"So?" she asked

'What next? Where you gonna take admission?' I asked

"H.M.V – Hansraj Mahila Vidhalaya." She said

It gave me a big jolt. I knew that college; it was an all girls' ccollege. There was no way I could have joined that college. (At least not with in the next two months! The sex change procedure was long. I knew that!!)

"Ok" I tried to remain calm.

"And…" she said

"And?" I questioned

'What about you? Where are you gonna go?' she asked

"O! Me! I am going to M.G.M PUBLIC SCHOOL. It's a co-ed you know." I said, looking down, playing with the pebble on the ground.

'Raj' she said

'Yes' I said, continuing to look down.

"Raj, look at me."

I looked up. With a face as upset as the ozone layer.

"And please smile." She continued "You look very cute when you smile."

I could not resist that.

"That is better." She said. "See, it's not the end. We will be in touch. Always."

I went home that day very confused – happy and disturbed.

The result was out. I was relieved about that. But Rushi!! Our friendship was very deep. I was very scared to lose it. I took the whole day to decide that she was the one, the girl I wanted to spend my life with. And I wanted her to decide the same. In the evening I called her.

"Rushi. Hi" I said. I was dead serious. And Rushi sensed it, just naturally - Without any effort.

"Raj, is everything ok?" she sounded concerned.

"Rushi, I love you. And I want you to be my girlfriend."

Silence

"I love you too Raj, but being your girlfriend, what will it change? Will it change the way we talk? The way we know each other? The way we are friends?" she asked, politely.

"No, it will not change all that. But it will confirm us being together. Forever." I said, with a trembling voice.

"Who knows what is to happen tomorrow Raj!" she said

"No one, But we can always plan. We *have* to plan!" I argued.

"Are you saying I should not go for a guy who I like more than you, if I meet him in the future. And as a matter of fact, the same applies for you!" she snapped. "What if you find a girl tomorrow, who you like more than you like me?"

"I know that will never happen."

"Raj," she said very seriously, "we are only 15!"

Silence.

"Raj, you are a very good friend of mine. *You are my best friend.* And I don't want to lose you *or* your friendship under any circumstances."

There was a pause for about five seconds. She took a deep breath and continued, "I hope this does not change the way we are Raj."

I was hurt, and embarrassed. I really didn't know what to say. But I knew one thing for sure – I couldn't have stopped talking to her, or have ended the relationship on the basis of what had just happened.

"No, it won't." I said firmly.

"Yes, and I will make sure it doesn't."

That was the first time I had proposed to her. And the first time she had said no.

My life becomes Dil To Pagal Hai.

The sky was overcast. The light was dim; the sounds of different birds could be heard. It was a very gloomy evening. Nisha was sitting on the shore, throwing pebbles in the lake, one after another. Looking at the water with unseeing eyes almost filled with tears. Rahul came and sat by her side silently. Without looking, she knew, it was him, she sensed his presence. She always could. She started to speak "*Mai achi ladki nahi hoon Rahul, mai bahut buri hoon.*" Continuing to throw the pebbles in the lake, with unseeing eyes, "*Nahi Nisha, tum meri dost ho, aur mera koi bhi dost, bura ho hi nahi sakta.*" Rahul said looking at her, trying to force a smile on his face.

"*Nahi rahul tum nahi jante,*" Nisha continued, "*ab dekho na, ek ladka hai, jis se mai bahut pyar karti hoon, aur aaj mujhe pata chala, ki who mujh se nahi, kisi aur se pyar karta hai,*" the sound of painful violins rose in the background, Rahul turned to look at Nisha, he realized that Nisha had discovered his deep and passionate love for Pooja, "*to mujhe acha nahi lag raha hai.. Mujhe aisa nahi lagna chahiye Rahul, mai bahut buri hoon.*" She struggled to say the last few words, as her voice cracked.

Rahul was listening to all this, and silently shedding tears. It was his turn to speak now. "*Nahi Nisha, tum buri nahi ho. bura woh hai*" he said, pointing to the sky, looking up, "*Woh ek ko doosre se pyar karvata hai,*" he said with a frown,

"*Haan, bura to woh hai, burato woh hai!*" Nisha got up and started shouting "*TUM BAHUT BURE HO! MAI NAHI! MAINE KUCH NAHI KIYA. SAB TUMHARI GALATI HAI SAB TUMHARI GALATI HAI!*" She started throwing pebbles towards the sky. Rahul went and held her hands. He stopped her from throwing the pebbles towards the sky, looked directly into her eyes and said, "I am sorry Nisha!"

They hugged, and held each other, tight. And cried their hearts out. This is a scene from *Dil To Pagal Hai*. I always felt that this was a very nicely handled scene. But I never knew one day my life will come soo close to this situation!

I was a baboon not to realize that Aksha had special feelings for me. I was a fool not to realize that all those phone calls every evening were not just because I was a very close friend. And all that extra special behaviour all the favours, all those soft, tender smiles were because of the special feelings she had for me. I was a donkey not to realize that all those expressions that used to surface when I used to tell her how many times I had proposed to Rushi and how I still felt that she was the one I wanted to spend the rest of my life with, all those were expressions of hurt.

These days I don't get any phone calls in the evenings. It is not that comfortable for us to hang around together anymore. Aksha finds it difficult to face every one, now that every one knows. But I still do go to CCD after office to relax for a few minutes. That day when I opened the door and entered the café I saw Aksha sitting on the sofa where I generally sit. I went there, "Hi!" I said, softly. She seemed lost; she looked up, "Hi." She replied.

"How come alone?" I asked.

"Just like that." She replied, staring at the table.

I sat next to her. "You all right Aksha?"

Just then my phone started to ring. The screen flashed **"RUSHI CALLING ..."**

I received the call. "Hey! Hi!! How are you?" Aksha turned around and looked at me, she knew whom I was talking to; there was only one girl who could bring that kind of zest in my voice.

"Hi! I have a good news to tell you!" Rushi said, sounding very happy.

"You are coming to Gurgaon!!" I said that in one shot, super excited.

"No stupid! I quit my job."

She was not happy with her present job, she had not got the kind of raise she was expecting, I knew that. But quitting her job was a good news??!!

"Because I got a new job!!! In SAP-LABS!!!" she sounded as if she was jumping.

I had heard of ADLABS. But what the hell was SAP-LABS? I had no idea. But from the sound of it, it was something big, and her getting a job there was a big reason to celebrate.

"All right then! When is the party?" I asked

"Very soon, very soon. Hey, I am still in office," she said "getting all my documents cleared up, and my piggy boss is staring at me like an owl, O MY GOD! I think he just heard what I said!! I will talk to you later! Bye!" she hung up.

I could not help smiling at the way Rushi was. I shook my head. I turned around to see Aksha sitting next to me, still staring at the table.

"I am a very bad person Raj, I am a very bad person." She said.

I looked at her with sympathy and empathy. "No you are not Aksha."

"No Raj, I am. You don't know." She went on, wiping her tears. "There is a boy. I have known him all these years. I love him. And I know he does not love me." There was a mounful silence or some five seconds. My heart felt to be beating louder and faster than I had ever felt it. "He loves someone else" she went on, "and whenever he talks to that girl, who makes her happy, I feel angry. I feel jealous. I am a very bad person Raj."

'No Aksha, you are not. You have not done anything wrong. You are not a bad person.' I tried consoling her. I do not have that good a way with words. I am just an ordinary Raj. No Rahul from *Dil To Pagal Hai.*

She wiped her tears, "Forget it," she said, and forced a smile "so, tell me, how was it today in office?"

"Not as bad as yesterday, I was not accused of committing any crime today."

She gave a little laugh.

"And, how was yours?" I asked

"Normal, like everyday." She smiled a little and wiped her tears again. "you know what, that stupid bubby, what she did today "

I go to an even bigger school.

A new school. A new beginning. Once again I was standing in front of a gate, M.G.M Public School Jalandhar, it read, towering over me. And I used to think my last school was big! God! I somehow managed to find the classroom and the section I had been allotted – 11th G. I could see a tallish, almost thin, wavy haired teacher standing inside the classroom. Asking everyone's names. He was smiling.

"May I come in sir?" I asked

He turned around and looked at me. Smiled. "You are most welcome." He was young, looked fresh out of collage. "What is your name?"

"Raj sir" I said

"Ok Raj sir, you can come in. I am your Math teacher."

Heh heh heh! My new Math teacher! Heh heh heh!

I was walking down the aisle looking for a seat when I heard this little girl trying to whisper to her partner, "My God! He is the only Raj in the whole non-medical section! Now I will have to get hold of him only!" Although she was trying to whisper, but well, lets face it! She was pretty loud. But I didn't really get what she was trying to say. I mean… "The only Raj"! What did she mean?

The teacher started the roll call. And suddenly I heard the name, Neelhans. !!!! What!!! Was she here!!!! The little girl who I had over heard *trying* to whisper said "present sir!"

Was it her? It had been such a long time. I didn't clearly remember her. After going home that day, the first thing I did – took out my childhood class photographs. Yes. It *was* she. The same face, the same eyes.

Next day when I went to school I was determined to go and talk to her. I knew someone in my new school!!

I went to school, kept my bag on my seat. That is when I heard some one calling me from behind.

"Scuse me, are you from the St. Joseph's Boys' school?" it was the girl sitting next to Hans the previous day.

"Yes" I said

"Hi, I am Deep, Deepmala Kaur. I am from St. Joseph's Girls' School. We should be friends!"

"Ok" I said.

"And also meet my friend," she pulled a hesitant, little Neelhans form behind. "Neelhans. She is also…"

"Are you the Neelhans from the St. Joseph's Jr. School?" I asked, with a smile.

"Yes" she replied, nodding.

"Hi! Do you remember me?" I asked.

"Yes, Raj from IV th standard. Whose name was put with my name in the lovers' list." She said. Still sounding a little angry about it.

"Ya, I am still very sorry about it."

There was a small pause.

"So, who is your favourite actor?" I tried to strike up a conversation

"Shah Rukh Khan." She replied.

"And actress?"

"Kajol."

"And favorite movie?"

"*Dilwale Dulhaniya Le Jaenge*" she said, shyly, looking down. Hmm, no wonder the strong fascination with the name.

That time I did not know that we three, Hans, Deep and me, we were gonna form this trio, who, for the next two years was going to have a blast in the school. And was going to fail! In every subject possible!

We pass naughty chits to each other in class and sing songs.

I was sitting at the New Delhi Railway Station. A cousin of mine had come to Delhi. He had a degree in computer engineering and had got a job in some big firm in Gurgaon. He is, by far, the politest guy I have ever known. So soft spoken that its not even funny! Has a voice, which is perfect for the job of a radio jockey. I was to receive him and drop him at the accommodation his company had arranged. Prateek, (that is his name) is tall, almost six feet, fair, almost as skinny as me and, one of the very few guys who I talk to, and respect. As soon as he got off the train, he handed me his ipod and all his luggage, informed me that he was suffering from a very bad tummy upset and rushed to the loo.

So, I was sitting there, on the huge pile of luggage, browsing through the songs he had in his flashy ipod touch. (I wished I had one!) Finally I found a song of my choice. Kim Wilde! The 80's pop icon! He had her whole collection! I chose a song at random *Forgive Me*. It goes something like this

What have you done to me?
What have you done to me? (Chorus)
I want you to forgive me.
What have you done to me? (Chorus)
Now is it time? To look further to the future

I was sitting on the platform, banging my head to the disco music. The train on the rails in front of me started to move.

The world, is sending an S.O.S to us all,

Is sending an S.O.S to call,

Is lost in confusion as she falls.

I want you to forgive me.

For all that it takes,

For all the mistakes

It's now that I want you to forgive me.

The train passed, leaving me visible to the people on the other platform. I felt someone staring at me. I looked up, across the rail tacks, on the other platform. The crowd parted. It was Neelhans. Still as short as she had been, still as innocent, with those big beautiful eyes. Standing there. Looking at me. I froze. It was actually her! The crowd thickened rapidly, and she got lost in it again. GOD!!! It was soo much out of *Veer Zara*, when Shah Rukh Khan sees Preity Zinta after all those years!!! I was soo overwhelmed! For the last six years, since the time I last talked to her on the phone, I had been trying to find her, time and again, only to fail. And that day I finally saw her. And didn't have the brains to follow her!! What an idiot I was! (I feel like slapping myself.) I felt a tap on my shoulder. 'Sir' it was Prateek. For some weird reason he always called me that. I always tell him that that he should realize that I am only one year older to him. And his counter argument was always that I should realize that he was one year younger to me.

"*Haan*?" I was shocked

"Is everything ok?" he asked.

"Ya, everything is fine absolutely, what can possibly go wrong? Its not that I saw my long lost girlfriend or something!" I said, all stammering and everything.

"...Not your girlfriend, you seem as if you have seen a ghost." Thank God! He didn't realize. He had no idea that I *had* just seen my long lost girl friend!

That day after dropping him to his destination I could not stop thinking about Neelhans. I remembered what her name meant   a blue swan, which was very rare, maybe existed only in legends. A blue swan that, had once been mine.

☞

Whenever I recall her, I picture her the same   just like Amrita Rao, as she was in *Ishq Vishq*. Mild mannered and soft spoken. Sensitive and caring, dreamy and romantic, always ready with the class notes for me, whether I asked her for them or not. Always wishing for things, that seldom happened.

It was nice in the beginning. We were very clear as to what we were going to become in future. I was to be an architect. Hans was to be a computer engineer. And Deep was open to all options – she would take up any course that she could get into! She was the freest of us all. I used to love going to her place in the evening. To see her cousins play, the naughty Karan and Ashima. They were in fourth and fifth standard that time I think. It used to be a treat, watching them Karan would come jumping and stand in front of Ashima and say

"Hi Barbie!"

And Ashima would shriek "Hi Ken!"

Then Karan would say, "Wanna go for a ride?"

"Sure Ken." Ashima would say, and they would both start dancing and singing '*I am a Barbie girl, in a Barbie world, made of plastic, its fantastic…*' seeing them, I used to get flashbacks of the time that I had spent with Mona when I was a kid.

Deep, Hans, and I were a trio all right, but Deep was always closer to me than to Hans. She was more experimental and freer and …well she was just more fun to be with! End of story!

All three of us used to love spending time with each other. We used to sit next to each other in the classroom. We used to have loads of fun, most of all in the math class. Deep, and me I could never get a single...digit of what he said! So we used to be busy passing small notes to each other that had stuff like,

$$"(A^2 + B^2) = ?"$$

And the next chit would say

$$"(A^2 + B^{2)} = B \ Busy"$$

Or if we were in a really naughty mood, the chits would say things like,

"Look at Megha sitting over there! All drooling over sir.
I am telling you, she is sooo in love with him!"

In such cases, the next chit would read something like,

"Well! He is a dish!"

Or

"Well...his mustaches are rather...cute."

That would be Deep by the way and not me! Or at times the chits would also read things like,

"I think I just saw the ghostly shadow of the principal outside.
We should stop passing the chits for a while."

Or

"I think sir just noticed us. We should chit-chat later."

Hmm! The days were super fun! Even after the day it happened – the first monthly exams. I had got a handsome 5 on 100 and Deep, a 30 on 100! Hans was good in math, she got a 55 on 100. And by the way, 5 was not the lowest score, there was a boy who had got 3 on 100. My math teacher, (who we had started calling iota by then, owing to his skinny appearance. Iota is $\sqrt{-1}$, which is like...almost nothing) was...weird! He didn't scream at me or shout at me. Instead, he called me and asked,

"Raj, I know you are a very bright student. What happened?"

I was speechless. He thought I was a very brilliant student. But after a while the truth escaped from my lips! I ended up saying, "sir, I don't like math, I don't understand it at all."

"See, this is what I wanted to hear! An honest answer!" he said with a sense of great achievement. "You are scared of the subject! All you need is a little practice. You are so quiet and attentive in the class. I was expecting a very good paper from you. I was shocked to see the way you have performed. Just work a little harder. And you will see that you perform wonderfully. And if at any point of time you need any help from me, just let me know. We teachers are always there to help our students. Ok?"

He was actually the nicest! Such a dedicated teacher! If Megha had been at my place, she would have either melted on the floor, or grabbed him wildly and kissed him and smooched him all over. I felt like giving a tight hug and saying 'thanx.'

I went back to a very hyper and excited Deep and Neelhans.

"What happened what happened? Are they demoting you!!! Shit! I had heard that they do so! But I could have never imagined in my wildest of dreams that they would to it with you!!! My god!!! What will we do now??!!" Deep was soo ... freaked out.

"Calm down, nothing of that sort..."

"Then" Deep interrupted me, "what did Iota say?"

"Nothing. He just told me to work hard."

"Really? O my god!!! I think I am falling in love with him! O god! But how will I remove that dodgy, bitchy Megha from my way; she will wear short skirts and win my sir's heart! O God! I will have to wear shorter skirts! Where will I get those from?!! Neelhans you got to help me with this...'

This is what we three did, all the time - had fun.

We were teenagers. And we were doing everything that teenagers did. From following the latest fashion trends set by the movie stars to chatting for long hours on the phone. We would call each other and talk for hours! The longest we ever talked was for 3 hours 45 minutes!!!! Yes! We used to talk for that long!! Beat that! On the phone Hans and me were unstoppable! What did we talk about? Well general stuff, what she did after school, what I did after school. Who was going around with whom in class. Who was failing, who was topping. Who would be the best source for the class notes, and who would we need to butter how for the same reason… the general stuff you know. But it was she only that used to call. She always used to tell me that her brother is generally on the phone and she would call whenever the phone would get free. One day I called her. Her brother picked up the phone.

"Hello" he said in his heavy scary voice

"Hello, can I talk to Neelhans?" I asked meekly

"Who is this?" he asked angrily

"Raj" I said

"Raj who?" he demanded

"…Her friend from school, …her friend…" I stammered

"Just a minute" he said. There was silence for a while, then I could hear him calling in the background "Papa! Some guy on the phone, says he is Neel's friend."

I gulped. Her brother sounded like a big tough huge guy.

"Hang on for a minute, I am coming." An even heavier voice said.

"Hello" it was her dad! He sounded even bigger then the brother! How could such a little girl have such huge brother and dad!

"*Namaste* uncle, I am Raj, Neelhans's friend, can I talk to her?" I said politely

135

"What do you want to talk about?" the questioned

"…The homework, I can't… remember…what they told us to do." I stammered going all red in the face.

"She is not home," he said, "I will tell her that you called when she comes back. And next time, listen to your teacher properly." The phone went dead after that – he had hung up.

That day I realized that her family was not ok with us talking on the phone.

Next day when she came to school, I asked her

"Your family has a problem if we talk on phone?"

She didn't reply, kept looking down.

"In that case Hans," I said with great dignity "we should not talk on the phone."

She looked up at me with an awfully sad face. Clearly there had been a very big scene about the phone call that I made the previous day.

She wanted to say something else, but she said, "Ok."

That time I didn't realize that it was primarily on the phone that I used to talk to Hans. During school hours, I would talk mainly to Deep.

After that day, things between us became a little strained. She started talking to me less. She would be sad most of the time. I remember asking her once what was wrong.

"I am very lonely Raj. And I don't know how to handle my loneliness." She said, with a serious, face.

"But, you have your family at home. And you have us in the school." I asked

"I cant explain it Raj, it… its like I feel all… empty…"

"Hans, is there a problem at home? Is your family troubling you?"

"No" she replied

"Are you sure?"

"Yes." She said.

Silence

"Is there any way I can help?"

Silence

"Hey! What you guys doing here? I been looking fo ya all over the place!" it was Deep showing off her newly acquired accent.

"Nothing," I said "I was just talking to Hans, it hurts me a lot to see her all sad like this." Hearing this Hans looked up at me. With Tears forming in her eyes.

"Uffo Raj, you also na! Its just… uff! Ok, she is all right. See she is smiling. Now here!" she placed three 3-star bars on the table, the cheap chocolate that we used to get from our school canteen, "have these. And lets hurry we are getting late for Mr. Aorta's class."

"Aorta?" I asked, "wasn't he iota?"

"Yes he used to be, but now I like to call him Aorta, something that is close to the heart, my heart." Deep said, trying to sound romantic in a completely filmy way.

"Deep, Aorta is not something that is close to one's heart, it's the name of a …"

"Uff! Now *you* don't start please. I am a non-med student and don't care about the medical stuff. Now hurry up, we are getting late!"

Mr. Aorta was on leave that day. So we got an extra sports period! The weather had transformed from harsh and sunny to a nice breezy and cloudy one. We were sitting in the football field, on the side benches, when someone said.

"Hey! Why don't we sing songs?! The weather is soo cool! It will really be fun!"

"Yeeeeeaaah!!" Everyone cheered!

"But what will we sing, …and who will sing?" some one pointed out.

"Neelhans will." Megha said. "I have heard people say she has got a very sweet voice."

"Yeah! Neelhans! Neelhans! Neelhans!" Everyone started cheering

"No no no no no!" Neelhans protested shaking her head. But some big tough boys came and pulled her up. And there she was, standing, with no idea as in what to do.

"What happened *Hans*?" Megha said, circling her like a hungry flying vulture or something, "can't you sing today? I have heard you have won quite a few singing competitions."

Silence.

She closed her eyes. Took a deep breath. And started,

> *Smile, your everlasting smile,*
> *The smile that brings you near, to me,*

She opened her eyes and looked at me, directly in the eye. She *was* a very good singer. I never knew her sweet voice was melodious as well.

> *Don't ever let me find you gone*
> *'Cos that would bring a tear to me.*
> *This world, has lost its glory*
> *Let's start a brand new story now, my love.*
> *You think that I don't even mean,*
> *a single word I say.*
> *It's only words,*
> *and words are all I have,*
> *to take your heart away.*

WOW! Was she great or what! I had no idea that she was such a wonderful singer!!! WOW! The cool wind running through my hair,

Hans standing there in front of me, looking at me, singing the song, all soo beautifully! I was stunned. Her sweet voice could have put a thousand nightingales to shame, could fetch clouds from the farthest corner of the world, could make a cool breeze blow, as soft and loving, as a mother's love for her child.

After she finished singing, most of the guys came and patted me on my back, as if congratulating me or something. For what! FOR WHAT!!! I didn't get it!!

...Crash! Boom! Bang!

It's been some time since I have told you what's up in office no? Well nothing really great happened that is worth mentioning; nothing till the day I am gonna tell you about now. When I went to office that morning, I was told that I was to go to this site and check some stuff. And how I was supposed to go? In the office Versa, which Kundan was to drive. Who is Kundan? Now, Kundan is this driver guy who tries his level best to look macho but ends up looking well, something weird. His heavy beer consumption has made him pretty ... pot bellied. He wears tight t-shirts and silver shades to look the way he wants to. (!!!) (Or may be not.)

According to me, the site was a 45 minutes drive, one-way. I gathered the stuff that I was to take and told Kundan that we were to go to this place. He looked at me, head to toe, and ... well it seemed he was thinking something, which I don't know, and I don't even care. I think he must have thought something like, "This weirdo, will he survive my versa ride?" Well whatever, I don't even care. Or maybe he thought that if he shook hands with me my bone in the forearm would snap or . Uh! I DON'T CARE! Anyways, he looked at me, thought something for a while, which I completely don't care at all about, and said, "Are we going now?"

"Yes," I said, "completely now."!!! What was wrong with me! What was I saying! May be it was something that gets induced into you when you are around such people.

Well I sat in the Versa, and within two minutes, I realized that his driving, was, seriously, not good for health! Sitting with him while he was driving, one could actually get a heart attack and DIE! While he was driving, the car remained in a constant state of acceleration, pressing me against the seat like a thin leaf, stuck on the windshield of an airplane flying at top speed, high up in the sky! I could not breath, felt like I was trapped in a vacuum! HE WAS DRIVING VERY FAST!!! I looked at him, he looked furious! As if he hated me or something. I closed my eyes and prayed to God! Tried to convince myself that it was all ok, I would survive. I told my self those golden words that the bell boy had once told Julia Roberts in *My Best Friend's Wedding*, sitting in the hotel corridor, outside her friend's room, - *like everything else, this too, shall pass*. The car screeched! And came to a sudden halt! Shocking! We were there! We had covered the 45 minute long journey in, well, guess what? 20 MINUTES! I calmed myself down and *did not freak out*. I stepped out of the car very coolly, trying to look all dignified and everything when I trembled and almost fell down. My legs were feeling rubbery, just like the way they feel when we step off a roller coaster.

It was just a 10 minutes' job on the site. Just 10 minutes' job and all that torture! But what was the point of cribbing. Had to go back in the same car anyways, so, I took all the necessary measurements and noted down all I needed to, went back, and sat on the seat, and strapped my seat belt, tight.

The car set in a constant state of increasing acceleration again. I kept telling myself its ok, it's all right. Soo many people have survived this. And so will I, so will I. Suddenly he turned the car, GOD! He turned the car at such a great speed! I felt I was gonna go flying out of the car, in the air, weeeeeeeeeeeeeeeeeee! I looked at him, it seemed he actually wanted me to go flying out of the car! I tried to calm myself down, trapped in that car with that maniac. Sitting there, having nothing really to do. I turned and looked at him again; he was not wearing his shades. The shades were lying right in front of me, on the dashboard! It was a great once in a lifetime chance to touch and feel and observe the ever popular 'Kunadan Shades'! I reached out and picked up the shades. I was holding the shades, IN-MY-HANDS! I observed closely, the silver shades, with wavy ear-hooks and super flashy nosepiece and rim. Suddenly I realized the car was accelerating at a rate way greater than it had been accelerating so far. I got scared, I kept the shades back, exactly the way they were kept before, at the same angle and position. The car started to slow down. THANK GOD! But for no good, suddenly a bull came, out of nowhere! Right in the middle of the road!

!!!!CRASH!!!!

!!!!BOOM!!!!

!!!!BANG!!!!

OUR CAR HIT THE BULL! OFF FLEW THE BULL! AND OFF FLEW OUR CAR!!! UPSIDE DOWN IT LANDED, THE WHEELS TURNING AROUND SLOWLY, WITH ME AND KUNDAN, IN IT, UPSIDE DOWN, STILL IN OUR SEATS! THANK GOD WE WERE WEARING SEATBELTS! I EXAMINED, I WAS FINE, BUT MY LEG, IT FELT ...

Hans seems to be psychic.

After that little song-singing day, things became even more weird between Hans and me. She would always tell me, "Raj, I want to talk to you about something." And whenever I would say, ok. She would try and struggle to say something, and go like "...may be sometime later". And start off with something like, "You know what! My dog Bozoe, he is chooo chweeeet! You know what he did yesterday..."

It took her, I don't know how many months, to finally talk about what she always used to say she wanted to talk about. It turned out that she wanted to tell me a story, about two friends – a guy and a girl.

"They were the best of friends. Knew everything about each other, shared all their thoughts and ideas about life. The guy always kept telling the girl that he wanted to tell her something. But every time she asked him what he wanted to tell her, he changed the topic. Years passed. They grew up. Got on with their lives, shaped their careers. But the guy still didn't tell the girl what he wanted to tell. One rainy evening he called her up. And told her that he wanted to meet her and tell her something. The girl said, "Fine, come over to my place!" They lived in a hill station. It was raining. Happily he tapped his fingers on the steering wheel to the music playing in his car as raindrops beat and elongated against the glass of the side windows of his car. Merrily his car drove on the serpentine road in the mountains. His personal diary was kept on the dashboard. In which he had written every thing about his friend. Everything, including how much he loved her. That day while driving, he met with an accident. His car fell in a gorge, with a loud crash it burst into flames. He died. And the girl, cried a lot at the loss of her friend. But she never got to know how much he had loved her. Cried for never getting a chance to tell him how much *she* loved him. So you see, you should always tell the other person about your feeling." She took a deep breath and repeated that part again, "And...

143

you should always tell the other person about your feelings. And I … yes. That is it."

!!! That was it?!!! This was what she always wanted to tell me!!! How did she know that I had a secret diary in which I used to write about Rushi? And did she have such a secret diary for someone?! She loved someone and she had never told me??!! Or she was trying to tell me that I was going to fall into a gorge the day I decide to show that diary to Rushi? Was she psychic? I didn't get it.

"So you see, one should never hide one's feelings from a friend." She repeated. Was she trying to say that I was hiding my feelings from Rushi? Well I *was not*! I had made every thing clear to her. May be much clearer than I should have. What was she trying to tell me?

One day, Hans looked upset. I asked Deep if she had told her anything about why she was so upset. She said, "Leave it no? She will be fine in some time. And you should not be so interfering you know. It is also possible that she might be having some girl problem." That time I never realized why she always was so uncaring about Hans, she was supposed to be her best gal pal. In the recess, Hans complained of a tummy ache and decided to stay in class. In the middle of the recess, after having our lunch, I went to keep Deep and my tiffin back in the class. I saw Hans scribbling something on a piece of paper. I quietly went behind her and snatched the paper from her. "What are you writing Hans? A love letter to your secret boyfriend?!!" I snatched the paper and ran to the corridor. "Raj! Give it back!" she shouted. I ran. Megha passed me; she could never keep her mouth shut! "What are you running away with Raj? Her *heart*?" that statement shook me. I stood there. Stunned. Slowly I straightened the paper in my hand.

144

Dear Raj,

Love does not happen often in life. And it is not always that the person, you love, loves you back. I love you. Yes I do. I have loved you since the day you first came to this school. I have loved you since the time I first talked to you when we were young. But I could never gather courage to tell you. I had always wished that my name in that lover's list was not a joke. I had always wished that you loved me back. But you never did, in the way I desired.

I can't stay here anymore. Stay here like this, dying everyday, being reminded how deeply I love you. And how I can never get you. I will not be coming to school from tomorrow onwards. I am leaving this city. I will be leaving for Dehradoon tonight. But I wish you love. And happiness. May you become the greatest architect.

With all the best wishes,

And all my love,

Yours, today and always,

Hans.

I had nothing to say. Suddenly everything started to make sense. Why Megha used to taunt. Why my classmates patted me like that the day Hans sang that song. Why Deep used to completely ignore Hans' behaviour – she knew. I realized what she was trying to tell me by telling that story of two friends. Everything became absolutely clear. I couldn't take it. I picked up my bag and went home. I walked through that corridor, with my bag on my shoulder. Sunlight was casting long slanting shadows in the whole length of the corridor. Hans stood there behind me with the letter in her hand and tears in her eyes.

I spend time reading and taking care of my broken leg.

... Broken! My leg felt broken! And it was my first facture ladies and gentlemen! And I was fully determined, to enjoy it to the fullest. But to my disappointment, it was only a green stick fracture, so; only 15 days rest. The doctor said I didn't really need a plaster, but I said, "no no! I do need! I *neeed* it! You must put the plaster on." And then there it was, my first plaster, And I was loving it! It was soo cool!

When my boss got to know, he was, well very worried, *that I was gonna take the next two weeks off*. He called me up.

"Hi Raj!" the sitar sounds.

"Hi boss", I replied

"It was very sad to hear what happened." Of course he was, he had lost a slave for the next two weeks! "Its terrible! The car will be in the garage for more than a week I think. How long does the doctor say that you are gonna take to recover?" WHAT! He was comparing my well being with his car! WITH HIS CAR!!!

"Two weeks boss, in a plaster."

"TWO WEEKS!" he almost screamed. "Which doctor are you seeing?"

I didn't feel like answering. But still had to say something. "My regular doctor boss, the one I go to every time I fall sick."

"You know something, I will tell you, go to my doctor; he is the best doctor in the whole of Asia! These days doctors you know, they exploit the patients! You may not need a plaster or that long a rest. And you know who my doctor looks like? James bond!" Bloody boss, wanted to keep a check on everything! I wanted my plaster! At all costs! And I would never let my boss *or* his doctor come in the way.

"Its ok boss. I will let you know if I need any help."

"Get well soon. That is all I can pray for to God." He said, sounding disappointed and helpless.

Huh! Pray for! MY FOOT!

I ended the call. Went home and was aahhhhh! I was relaxing in my bed! *Actually* relaxing after such a long time! Doing nothing, just lying in my bed and relaxing!" Someone knocked on my door, "COME IN." I said. It was Manisha, with fruits and flowers in her hand. She must have got to know through office.

"I just thought I should get some *phal* and *phool* for you." She said. O! That delicate beauty of hers! That ever-gorgeous smile! And those pink gerberas in her hand, with grapes and oranges! Picture perfect I tell you! "So", she came and sat next to me on the bed, "Our Mr. Painter got hurt."

"Yes and now Mr. Painter can finally take a break from that sick office!" I said

"Hey! You should not think like that. It's a very nice office. Boss may say or do things, which may not be the most appropriate, at times. But the office does support you at many levels and we should be grateful for that."

"Ok, as your highness says." I was in no mood to waste even a minute of my precious time by talking about the stupid office.

"But first thing's first, here," I gave her a permanent marker, "you got to sign on my plaster." And so she did. She wrote,

> *Dear Raj! You are the bravest of all,*
> *I want to see you jumping and hopping'*
> *The way you always do.*
> -Manisha

She signed her name, and made a very cheerful smiley, and a flower with that.

"Hey! I got these books for you." She placed three books by my side on the bed *Where Rainbows End* by Cecelia Ahern, *If You Could See Me Now* by Cecelia Ahern and *Trust Me*, by Rajashree. "These are three very light and wonderful books, pleasant and nice. I am sure you will enjoy them."

"Manisha, you shouldn't have. I already have such a huge pile of books lying here," I said pointing at the huge pile of books lying on the table on my side, "which I keep buying all the time whenever I go to the malls."

She looked at the books, "Hmm, Marian Keyes, Meg Cambot, Sophie Kinsella, Srividya Natarajan, and bodybuilding for beginners ! I am sure you are gonna like the books that I got you." She smiled, and I smiled back. "I never knew that you were into weightlifting and bodybuilding" she said.

"I don't, it's just that once in a while ... I try lifting some weights " I said, going all pink in the face!

"O god! What's the time?" she asked nervously

"It's 8.30"

"God! I am late! I am really sorry Raj but I really got to rush."

"No problem, I am really delighted that you came. Do drop in again."

"I will. And get well soon. Bye." She left. I put on my glasses, and lying on my bed, opened one of the books that she had got for me *Trust Me* by Rajashree, the first line read, "all men are Bastards " it really intrigued me. The book was about a girl working in an ad agency as an art director and struggling hard to get over the heartache that her ex boyfriend had given her by. I had hardly read some five pages of the book when I heard someone banging hard on the door.

"COME IN"

It was Guneet with Shalini and Aksha.

"O! My! God! *Phal, phool aur kitabain!*' Guneet exclaimed, "who got these for you Raj? Your secret girlfriend?"

" No " I blushed, "it was Manisha."

"O my God! So it was your secret girlfriend!"

" No. I ... "

"And what is this?! You started body building?! You never told me Raj!" she said, looking at me from head to toe, not missing to check out my biceps and trying to peep into my shirt, which had its top three buttons open. "Hmm, and with some *little* results, I see." I was turning all red! I started to button my shirt

"Ok don't waste my time, give me a marker; I can see that Manisha has already sighed at the exact spot where I wanted to. I don't want to lose the next spot." I handed her the marker, she started doodling, a caricature of me with leg plastered and all. "And what book you reading *haan*? *Trust Me*?" she said, as she continued drawing, "Who gave *this* to you *haan*?"

I didn't reply. I was busy going all pink to red to crimson to God knows what.

"Anyways, here", she gave the marker to Aksha, "you both should also sign. You broke your leg on such short notice Raj, we could not take out much time, we can't spend much time with you today. But will definitely spend the whole evening with you tomorrow. We got to rush now, have some work. See you tomorrow. *Get up you girls!*" she said looking at Shalini and Aksha. And they left.

⌒

Next day, early morning, around 7 O'clock, there was another knock on the door.

"COME IN"

"Hi" Aksha entered, holding a bouquet of flowers. She held the most beautiful of flowers in the clumsiest manner. Blue Orchids, white gladioli, and white lilies.

"Hey! Hi! Come, come. So nice to see you so early in the morning!" I welcomed her.

"How are you feeling now?"

"I am all right."

"I got flowers for you."

"Ya, thanks! These are beautiful."

She sat down, on the edge of the bed, and smiled. She had a look of satisfaction on her face   I had liked the flowers, and was happy to see her.

"Two weeks, the doctor says, right?" she asked.

"Ya" I confirmed.

Silence.

"How's your office going?" I asked.

"Fine."

I was finding it difficult to strike a conversation.

"Does it hurt really bad?" She asked softly

"No," I chuckled, "not when I am talking painkillers- The KILLERS! GGRRRRR!" I growled, jokingly, like a hungry tiger or something

She smiled.

Silence.

"You stay alone Raj, how are you gonna manage?"

"Its ok Aksha, I will. I always have."

"If you need anything, at any time, please, let me know."

"I will." I said.

She looked at her watch, "I am getting late for my office, I have to leave" she got up.

"Ok" I said.

"Take care, and get well soon."

"Thanks, and you too, take care."

She smiled, and left.

At around 8.30, there was another knock.

"COME IN"

"Haanji sir! How are you?" it was Prateek, with pomegranates in his hands. I completely failed to understand how everyone was getting to know about my accident! Had they all fixed some spy camera in my room or something??!! O my god! Did that mean that they could see everything I did in my room??!!

"Prateek! Hi! Its soo nice to see you! How are you?!"

"I am fine but look at what you did to yourself! You must be more careful."

"Yeah I know!" I sighed. "So tell me, how is your new job going?"

"Fine. Hey! What is this, you have started bodybuilding?!"

Uff! That book I tell you! I felt like throwing it away; send it out flying out of the window! "No. Not really." It was embarrassing, a stick figure like me, possessing a bodybuilding book. "So, were you able to find decent accommodation for yourself?" I tried to change the subject.

"No," he answered, "and I wanted to talk to you about it. I have been trying to find a decent place, and have not been able to find any. Can I move in with you? That is, if there is no problem and if you don't mind?"

Patience pays!!!! I did have a spare room in the flat where I was staying, alone. All these years of staying alone finally paid off!

151

God finally sent a decent roommate for me!!!!! Some one who I could stay with! Someone who I didn't find annoying!

"*MIND*? I would love it if you stay here!"

"Thanks!"

"No problem buddy!"

The rest of the days went real cool, with Prateek in the next room who would come running whenever I called him to fetch me anything I needed, and reading all those wonderfully funny books, with my glasses on.

A new love blooms.

I went home that day and tried my level best not to think about the thing that I was completely consumed with. I turned on the television. *Bridget Jones' Diary* was on, one of my all time favourites. I love watching the super sweet, unattractive, fat, super confused Bridget. It's towards the end of the film, that one of her friends makes her realize and says, "*Bridget! He loves you, just the way you are!*" As a stunned wide eyed Bridget stares back, realizing, that Mark Darcy loved her, just the way she way, without any change! JUST THE WAY SHE WAS! And then it hit me! Hans! She loved me! THE WAY I WAS! *JUST* THE WAY I WAS! I still tried to run away from the feeling, I changed the channel "*Pyar! Pyar dosti hai. Agar wo meri achi dost nahi ban sakti toh…*" Shah Rukh dressed in a super tight t-shirt was putting forward his idea about love, *Kuch Kuch Hota hai*. I could not run away from it anywhere, God was showing me all the signs. My heart started pounding; now it was a race against time, she was leaving town tonight, and it was already 6 O'clock! I picked up the phone and dialled her number, fingers crossed and praying to God that *she* picks up the phone! Not her brother, not her father, but she, herself!

"Hello!" THANK GOD! IT WAS HER!!!

"Hello…" what was I to say next?! WHAT?!

"Raj?" she said, as she sniffed. She sounded as if she had been crying all day.

"Yes, …hi! …How are you?" I asked

"I am fine."

Silence.

"Hans, I want you to stay."

Silence.

"And why is that?" she asked

"I want you to stay … so that I can be with you." That was the best I could come up with!

"You want me to stay," she sniffed again, "so that you can be with me? Please explain."

"Now come on Hans, … I know you know what I mean."

"I know. But are you sure?"

"Yes I am." I said.

"Then why can't you say so?" she demanded.

"Because… I can't."

"If I can, then why can't you?" she questioned.

"Well! It was easier for you! You *wrote* it!"

"Excuses, excuses! That is what you always offer Raj." I could almost see her frowning on the other end of the line.

What the hell, if I was feeling it, then why couldn't I say it? "Ok, FINE, I love you."

Silence.

"I love you too." Her voice shaky, she was crying again. Girls I tell you! Happy or sad! They will always cry!

From that day on, we started going around officially.

The following days were very pleasant. We started meeting secretly, in the only fast food joint in Jalandhar (at that time that is) – Heat 7. We would exchange gifts and cards. I would give her books like Eric Segal's *Only Love*, and music compilations like *lessons in love*. She would give me flowers (artificial, so that they would last forever) and books like *Pride and Prejudice*. I still remember that day! God! We were at Heat 7, had gifts for each other in our hands, packed with love, paper and ribbons. Sitting there, talking to each other. I was more that alarmed when I saw Ravinder Aunty enter the restaurant and sit in the other corner.

"Hans! That aunty over there! She is our neighbour!" I exclaimed.

"Shit!" she exclaimed

"God!" I exclaimed

"What should we do?" She exclaimed. We both lowered our heads, as if that would help us hide ourselves.

'......' I was petrified! If she saw me sitting there with Hans, the next day the whole colony would know that I had a girlfriend and was meeting her, *alone*, these days!

After a while, Hans and I could not help laughing at the situation! We were... worried and ... laughing.

"Imagine! If my brother gets to know!" she said. "I will be soo dead!"

We were hysterical! We let the aunty leave before us.

The news reached my home before I could. My mom already knew. "So, you have a girlfriend hmm?" she asked with a naughty smile.

'......'

"Come on don't be shy, tell me, what her name is?"

"Come on now, tell me, or I will call up and ask Deep. ...Or is it...Deep?"

"Hans." I said, going all pink.

"Oooo! Hans. She is a nice girl, I like her." She looked at me and smiled, enjoying seeing me blush. "You are a big boy now. And can take your own decisions. And I have full faith and confidence in you. I know you will never make a wrong move, or do something that is harmful for you, your health or your future." That is it. That is all she said.

Soon it was time for the 12th standard boards. And then, for the entrance tests, then, for the results, after that for the admissions. Deep got admission in B.Sc in Computer Science in Layalpur Khalsa Collage Jalandhar. Hans decided to do B.C.A and took admission in APEE JAY Collage Jalandhar. I decided to go to Gurgaon, to study architecture, in Sushant School of Art and Architecture. With time things change. Relationships became distant. And that was what was happening.

It was a very gloomy evening. The rain had just stopped an hour ago, still leaving its taste hanging in the air. Everything looked damp and old, the school building looked decadent thickly covered with mess that had grown on it during the recent rains. The sky was gray, covered by a thick cloud. Lightning and thunder still threatened to send a strong shower down any instant. Hans and I were standing under a bottlebrush tree in the school garden. The tree was in full bloom, beautiful read flowers all over, which to us seemed to have been dipped in blood that had been painfully drained out of our hearts.

We were standing there in silence, looking down.

"When are you leaving?" she finally broke the ice.

"Next Friday."

"…And when will you come back?" she asked.

"I don't know. May be sometime next month." My throat felt dry.

"I am gonna miss you."

Silence.

"Raj," she looked up, "please don't forget me when you go to your new college." She dropped her head again, she was crying, I knew.

"Hans, look at me," I held her shoulders, "I love you. And will always do. You don't have to worry about anything I will always be yours. I will always love you."

"I know you do Raj, but those Delhi girls, you don't know them, I know, …I have cousins in Delhi, girls there wear micro minis and tempt boys and make them fall in their traps of fake love, use their money and…offer them…their bodies…. And use them …and do stuff with them and them just …to satisfy their own urges and…"

"Hans, I am not gonna fall for any such girl, I am not gonna fall for any such slut. I know how the world is. They can not take me away from you."

She smiled for two seconds, with tears in her eyes, then sadness took over her face again.

We hugged. The cold chilly wind kept blowing, constantly. That day, I decided, Hans was my girl. And I made up my mind to leave Rushi.

Part 3

Part 3

I say no and then I say yes.

We had been in the train for F-I-V-E H-O-U-R-S! And still not there! There was no sign of Delhi still. DELHI WAS *FAAAAR*! My mom, dad and I were travelling to Delhi, in Shaan – e – Punjab, AC chair car.

'I am not joining this college in Gurgaon.'* I declared. As if it was my final verdict.

My mom smiled. "And why is that, if I may ask."

"*Mom*! It has been five hours and we are still not there! It is *far*! How will I come back on the weekends? This is not working. I am not gonna study there."

My mom looked at me, naughtiness bubbling in her eyes, "Ok, so where do you want to study?"

"I don't know, Chandigarh! Or Amritsar maybe! That seems closer!"

"Ok."

---

* For the people who don't know – Gurgaon is a town, which is right next to Delhi, which is now a part of the N.C.R – the National Capital Region of India. So if you have to go to Gurgaon, it is most convenient to go through Delhi.

161

"Ok what! We are not going there! We are going back!"

"Ok, but we can't jump out the moving train, right? Once we reach the Delhi Railway Station, we will take the next train to Jalandhar." She said, as coolly as I don't know what, quietly sipping her tea.

After a total of more than six hours, we reached Delhi. The station! My god! Soo many people! O God! I tell you! Soo many people would not have been there in the whole of Jalandhar! And here they were! All of them! At one, single, railway station! There was no place to move. We were stuck! We just had to move with the crowd, or rather, run, yes, run is more like it, we had to run with the crowd. This is how the city is actually isn't it, when you come here first you get stuck in the city, and then, in order to survive, you have to run, run and …keep running. And I had never been the kind of person who likes to run, or like speed for that matter. I like to walk. And in this city, if you try to walk, people come from the back, push you, leave you lying on the ground, and trample over you!

It was a great battle, but finally we won! We were out of the Station! With all our luggage intact!

"So, lets make arrangements for the tickets back to Jalandhar" my mom said, looking at me tauntingly.

"…Can't we see a little bit of Delhi. The Qutub Minar, or the Gateway of India maybe." I said, in a very hesitant voice.

She smiled. "Ok ji!" she turned around to my dad, "your son wants to see Delhi. Now what can I do about it."

And that day, we went to see a little bit of Delhi. And that day, I finally learned! THE GATEWAY OF INDIA WAS IN *BOMBAY*, AND *INDIA GATE* WAS IN DELHI!

Delhi is a very big city. That is what I had always been told. It had tall buildings and more cars on the roads than you could count. And it was true. All the people that we saw in the movies like *Shaan* etc. –

crippled people, sitting on boards with rollers and all, they were all actually there! On the traffic signal, on the roadside… It was a very different kind of a place. I was overwhelmed.

"So, you have seen all that you wanted to." mom said

"Yes."

"Should we go back now?"

'………'

"We can stay a little longer, and go to see the college that you were supposed to join."

"…I guess." Putting on a fake expression of disappointment.

It took us another hour to reach that college. It was even further! Way ahead! Sector 55, Sushant School of Art and Architecture – in the wilderness, completely out of the city. A long straight road led to the place, on the sides of the road there was nothing but dense shrubs. I was lucky to spot a few *neel gai* on the way. The college was in the middle of nowhere. It had a vast desert like flat land with some sturdy trees and shrubs on one side, and a long seemingly endless rocky ridge on the other side. * I could see the college building from like a distance of …5 km. *It was that desolated!****

The new shining, neat college building stood very confidently in the middle, with its head held up high.

"So," my mom said, "are you gonna study here?"

And I said… "Yes." It was beautiful.

** The ridge mentioned here is a part of the Aravali foothill rage.
*** Gurgaon was a completely different place back then.

Someone comes back!

Guess what happened today!!! Pragya joined our office!!! It's not good you know, for her, looking at how much the office sucks. BUT! I have a close friend working in office now!!! Yeaaaahhhhh!!! O! Wait a minute; I have told you who Pragya is right? No? Ok, I will tell you who Pragya is. Well, Pragya is a very close friend of mine. She is from the same collage as I am. But in collage we never interacted much. She used to be this tall, thin, long legged girl who wouldn't talk much to anyone. I will tell you the day when we actually started talking.

It was one of my college friend's boring birthday party. You know, the kind where everyone gets together and drink and smoke and nothing more. I was bored to the bone. So I went out for some fresh air. I stood there was a few minutes, feeling the cool breeze of the night. Pleasant it was, I was refreshed. But I didn't feel like going back to the party. As always the party was in one of the pubs in Mega Mall. I turned around trying to decide what to do whether to go back or not. By chance my eyes caught the sight of a signboard Café Coffee Day. Ha Ha Ha! All confusions gone!

I opened the CCD's glass door and guess what? I saw a very chirpy and happy Pragya sitting inside. She had all the waiters standing around her, clapping for her when she was cutting a chocolate fantasy with ice cream. Was it her birthday? And why was she celebrating it alone?

"YEAAAAAHHHH!!!" she looked all happy as she cut the cake.

I went to her. "Hi" I said.

"Haaaeeee! How are you! Long time! You just simply vanished after college?!" that is how it is for everyone isn't it? Vanish after college, disappear into the crowd of the world, and get lost, and lose identity.

"I am fine. Ya. Happy birthday."

"Its not my birthday," she said quickly in one breath, putting a big piece of cake in her mouth.

"Then why are you cutting a cake?"

"O! This! Coz the results are out. Again."

"And?" I asked, getting all ready to congratulate her.

"I FAILED AGAIN!!!! YEAAAAHHHH!".

"Ok." I did not know what to say.

"We should celebrate our failures. They are the stepping-stones to success." She said, waving and nodding to all the waiters standing around.

"Ok." I said

"Why are you so lost?" she asked. "Come, sit." She patted on the seat next to her.

"Ok." And I sat next to her.

"So, how is life?"

"Life is cool, Normal."

"hmm" she said, as if she was thinking something, "is that how my life is gonna be once I clear all my subjects? In that case it is all the more reason to celebrate the fact that I failed!!! I get more time to enjoy college!"

"Yes" I said "so, how's college?"

"O SHIT! I HAVE TO PICK UP THE CLOTHES FROM THE DRY CLEANER! AND THE SHOP CLOSES AT 8:30! AND I CANT GO TO THE DISK WITHOUT THOSE TOMORROW!" She exclaimed. "Can we go to my flat and talk there?" she asked.

I didn't really know her well then. I don't know why but I said, "ok." Maybe coz I didn't have anything better to do that time.

I get busy! (With college).

Once again it was time to start everything afresh – a brand new beginning, in a new city, where no one knew me. I was allotted a room in the hostel. It was time for my parents to leave me, and go back home. There we were, standing outside the hostel, mom and dad, all set, to leave me and go.

The sky was partially covered with white candyfloss clouds. My mom's blue chiffon *dupatta* was as always playing with the wind, wishing me good luck.

"Take care of yourself my son. Now I am not gonna be around." She said, smiling. I nodded, looking down at the ground.

My dad stepped forward. He hugged me tightly.

"Take care of yourself son, and if there is any problem of any kind, just let us know." His voice was shaky, he looked different. I always knew he loved me. But at that time, at that spot, …well I can't really express, but all I can say is after that day; I loved, and respected him, a lot more.

I stood there, watching them go in that black and yellow taxi. Slowly the car vanished, out of my sight. I took a deep sigh and I went back to my new room. Where everything was new. Nothing looked familiar. Nothing looked mine. No people, no objects, nothing. And now that my mom and dad had also left, I knew no one at all. The room was empty. Standing in the doorway, I took one look from one corner of the room to the other. I went and sat on the bed and ran my hand on the fresh bed sheet mom had had so tidily spread, looking at the small yellow flowers and green leaves, and the bands of green lines it had printed on it, I took a deep breath. And guess what! I cried! But not much just like for some three minutes. Then I wiped my tears away, and started preparing my stuff, for my first day in college.

College turned out to be louder than I had imagined. Most of the guys had long hair and most of the girls, short hair. Guys found great pride in telling others that they were gay and girls found even a greater pride in saying that they were lesbians. Almost everyone had studs and pierced body parts! (At the most weirdest of places!) Every one seemed to wear soiled and dirty clothes. And looked as if had not slept for years! It was difficult to locate a guy / girl without a cigarette in hand. Architecture colleges I tell you. Seniors were seniors; they ragged us beyond limits, but the teachers! Well! They were worse! Sick, dying, broken leg, 104 fever, whatever may be the case, you had to come for the classes and YOU HAD TO GIVE THE SUBMISSION. Failing the students was no big deal for them.

The first person I talked to in the college was Shweta Srivastav. I saw her in the hostel bus in the morning. We got down from the bus and I saw going towards the first year studio.

"Hi, my name is Raj. First year architecture?"

"Yes. Hi. I am Shweta."

"Where are you from?"

"Dehradun. You?"

"Wow! That is a cool place. I am from Jalandhar."

"Ok. Do you know the way to the first year studio?" she asked

"Yeah, its this way." I led her. "Is there any other architecture first year student in the girls' hostel, there isn't any in the boys'."

"Ya, there is Guneet. You have not met her? She is very hard to miss." She giggled a little.

"Ok, where is she from?" I asked.

"She is from Chandigarh."

"O! There she is! GUNEET! HI! HERE!" she waved out to a girl standing at a distance, looking more lost that anyone else around. And trying her level best not to look lost.

"Hiiiiiiii!" she almost screamed, and came running.

"And who is this new…" she asked Shweta.

"Hi! I am Raj. I am from Jalandhar." I said, extending my hand.

"Hi! How skinny and nerdy could someone get!" she said, almost laughing, as we shook hands. I WAS OFFENDED!

"Come lets go," Shweta said, "we are getting late for the class, Raj knows the way."

"Yes yes, I also know." Guneet said.

We stood there like for five seconds and then I said, "its this way."

"Yes yes, I know" and Guneet started walking towards some other corridor.

This is how we met, to be the thickest of friends for so many years to come. We had a weird chemistry, all three of us. Guneet and I would always get hyper over the smallest of the matters, and fight, and Shweta would be the neutralizing factor. Just the way she was on the day we first met. *

I didn't even realize how a full month passed and it was time for our first group assignment. We were to form a group of six and do some work. Guneet, Shweta and I were to be together. But we needed three more people. Now there was this girl, Aksha. According to Guneet

---

* And where is Shweta Shrivastav now, you would ask. Well she is in Cardiff doing her masters. So don't think or ask again. And by the way, she is not the Shweta who is my work colleague; she is a completely different Shweta. It's just that Shweta is a common name, and I have more than one Shweta in my life.

and Shweta she was a very nice girl. But I was not so sure. According to me she was the girl who would sit on the front seat in the class, and not share anything with anyone, no pencil, no eraser, no cutter, nothing. Not even a tracing sheet. I remember, once we were having our art and graphics class and I was out of tracing sheets, I saw some sticking out of Aksha's portfolio lying next to her drafting table. I went to her and asked, "Hi, can you lend me a tracing sheet?"

"I don't have any to spare." She said, tucking her fresh, blank, EXTRA tracings inside her portfolio. I DID *NOT* LIKE HER. But Guneet and Shweta insisted. And who can stand up against Guneet you know. So I said, 'Ok! *Fine*! Lets have her!'

Aksha came with two free gifts – Shalini and Shilpa.

I liked Shilpa and Shalini. Shalini was this no nonsense girl but would completely enjoy all my non-sensical jokes I would crack all the time. And Shilpa was this little super active humming bird, soo bubbly and chirpy that it was hard to believe.

"So Raj, you from Jalandhar right? And you have a girlfriend back there as well, right?"

I had spilled the beans once while I was being ragged. "Yes." I said.

"And you gifted her '*Lessons for Love*' right?" Shilpa inquired

"Yes."

"How *sweet*! I wish I had a boyfriend who would give *me* '*Lessons for Love*' haaaannnn!" she said, with super dreamy eyes.**

"What is her name?" She went on.

"Neelhans." I replied, with a straight face.

"How ceuuuute!"

"Yes, and we are going very strong. I love her very much."

** HOW SWEET?!!!! I WHISH I HAD A BOYFRIEND WHO WOULD GIVE ME LESSONS FOR LOVE?!!! WAS SHE THE GIRL MY HANS HAD WARNED BE ABOUT??!!!!

"But long distance relationships, seldom work yaa. When was the last time you guys met?"

"It was quite some time back. But that is not a problem; we guy understand each other. We have very good understanding. She know I love only her, and no one else. And am not or neither will ever be interested in any other girl. I am a one woman guy." I said looking a her, frowning.

'That is really nice, you should take care.' Shilpa said

'I do take care. Thank you very much.'

And that is how our tight group of friends got complete.

I hang up the phone on one girl, put my head down for ten seconds, and then call up another girl.

How busy the college was? Well, I did not get time to realize or assimilate my thoughts about the idea. COZ IT KEPT ME SOO BLOODY BUSY! I was not able to go home and meet Hans on the weekends as I had promised. I used to talk to her on the phone, on alternate days or so after collage. As soon as I would get off from the bus, I would head straight to the market, to the nearest yellow coloured S.T.D P.C.O and call her.

She was getting a little insecure (A little! Well that is an understatement, a lot; she was getting *a lot* insecure). During our past soo many phone calls, we had primarily fought and not been able to have a decent conversation, leave aside having sweet talks of loooove.

"Why wont you come home Raj?" she said. I knew that tone. She was crying.

"Hans, I can't. I have too much workload here yaar, there is a submission every Monday. I have not slept properly in weeks. I have not slept for more than three hours per night for I don't know since how long now." I tried to explain.

"Is it work that keeps you up all night or is it something else?"

I was furious. "What do you mean?"

"Your group work and night stay *ka bahana* Raj, I know every thing, it can not go on like this."

"Go on how Hans?" Now she was being really unreasonable.

"I am asking you straight Raj. If you have another girl there, just tell me."

Silence.

"I don't want to be left hanging in the middle. I want to be either here or there." She continued.

Silence. I should have hung up. But I didn't.

"Hans, if we don't even have this much faith and understanding, there is no point of carrying this relationship any further." I said in the most serious tone ever.

"I knew this. Why cant you be a man about it and SAY IT, that you have found another girl there."

"You know what Hans, may be I am NOT A MAN! May be that is the reason I have been saying no to all the sexy girls around me!"

Silence.

"Bye Hans." And I hung up. I put my head down on the table for some ten seconds, then I dialled another number.

"Hello, Rushi?"

"Hi!! Such a looong time! Where were you? And where *are* you? I am in Jalandhar, doing computer engineering. We should meet up some time!"

"Yeah, I am in Gurgaon these days …"

That was the last time I ever talked to Neelhans. After that day, she vanished. She left the college, the city, everything. I still don't know where she is.

I go yaaaa! And then I go hmmm!

My friends were more than sad to know that I had broken up with Hans. Then they were more than happy to know that I had started talking to Rushi again.

"What is she like?"

"Do you have any picture of her?"

"What is her favourite colour?"

"What is her favourite outfit?"

Guneet, Shilpa, Shweta, Aksha, fired a volley of questions at me.

"She is a fun person to be with. No I don't have any picture of her with me. Her favourite colour is yellow. Yes, we both like the same colour for the same reason, for symbolizing happiness. And like everyone else, she finds herself most comfortable in jeans and t-shirts. Now can we get back to work?"

We were all at Aksha's place. There was a major submission the next day. A few packets of different flavours of potato chips along with a few 500ml bottles of Coke, Pepsi and Fanta were lying on the floor next to our drafting boards. It was way beyond midnight and all normal human beings were fast asleep. Not a single soul was out on the roads. While inside, we were busy chatting and gossiping. This was a normal general working night of our college days.

"We should do something to get in touch with Rushi more no?" Shilpa asked Aksha with a frown.

"Yes", she replied in a low voice.

"What's her sun-sign?" Shilpa asked.

"She is a Virgo." I replied.

"Perfect match! You are a Taurean, she is a Virgo! Perfect I tell you!" Shilpa exclaimed.

"What's her e-mail id?"

"I am not telling you that. Now can we get back to work?"

"Guys, its 4:30 in the morning already and we have a submission at 9:30. There is loads of work still left. I think we should concentrate on our work." A very worried Shalini said. While we all were chatting away to glory, she had been sitting in a corner, working quietly.

'Yaaaaa' we all said in full synchronization, as if we all had been hypnotized. Working in the night it makes you a little crazy.

Staying with Prateek was turning out to be really cool. It was nice to stay with the guy, who would wake up early in the morning to perform his yogic *asanas*, then go for a jog, then get ready and go for his job, come back even later than me in the evening. AND NEVER CRIB FOR EVEN A SECOND! After he came back, we would go to the near by *Romi Ka Dhaba* to have dinner.

"So, how was your day in office?" I would ask Prateek.

"Normal, hectic, nothing special."

He never failed to amaze me. How could he so easily and coolly say, normal, hectic !?

"Don't you ever get frustrated or fed up at office?" I questioned.

"Not really."

"How long have you been working?"

"Two months."

Ah! That was why!

"But sir, I think the key to keep such frustrations away, is not to

174

think too much about it." He said tearing his *roti*. "Not to think too much about office, and by not to getting involved in office, but getting involved in work."

"Hmmm." I said, chewing the food in my mouth. I had a lot to learn from this guy. Hmmm.

I paint Pragya.

It was Pragya's first day in office. And I had made her a present. I told her that after office she would have to come with me to my place as I needed her help for something I was doing. We parked the car. I blindfolded her.

"Come", I took her by her hand and led her to my flat, holding her hand we climbed the stairs. I took her to my room and opened the blindfold. She was standing there, facing the wall that I had covered with huge curtains, red velvet curtains, with golden border. Full theatrical style!

"Wait, stand here." I went and pulled the curtain.

The curtains parted, to reveal the painting of her.

She kept standing there. Did not move. Did not say anything.

I call this The Monsoon Goddess. "This is how I have always seen you. Smiling, cheerful, dancing."

She went closer to wall, to have a closer look at the painting. O my god! Did I do something wrong? Did she hate it! Did she think I had painted her ugly! God! Had I offended her! God! Was she gonna slap me and just storm out of my house! She turned around, o my God! Here it came! My first slap from Pragya! I shut my eyes. She hugged me.

"O Raj! It is soo beautiful! Thank you soo much!"

"You like it?"

"Like it?! I *love* it! And I love it soo much that we should celebrate!" she said taking the painting off the wall. I had just planned to show her the painting. Not to give it to her, I was to put it in my room.

"Pragya", I said, with hesitation, "this was to show you, not to give you."

"Whatever, I like it, so I am gonna take it."

"But "

"Shup! Pragya likes it, Pragya takes it."

I get my new spiritual guru.

It was really nice and inspiring staying with Prateek. I started getting up early and jogging. My next five weeks plan included start doing yoga. Each day I was learning something new. Every evening he would come back. All happy and not tired. And he would come to me and say, 'haanji Sssir! Dinner karne chale?' and off we would go to have dinner.

Dinnertime was turning out to be a series of super enlightening spiritual classes. My super enlightenment spiritual classes under the dim light of that hanging bulb, in that noisy dhaba, where most of the guys around were truck drivers, who would keep saying things like, "Oye teri maa di , or Oye teri bhain di and other stuff like that, I would sit there on the charpoy, and take lessons from my new, very own yo-spiri Guru who's mind, body and soul were completely intuned with the cosmic powers of the world that we all live in. BOOM PRATEEK!

Once I remember, we got talking about how we dream all our lives and when these dreams do not come true, unhappiness is born. To this he said, "we should not get unhappy about our dreams not becoming a reality. As life, is nothing; but a series of experiences. And we live two lives, that is, we have two series of experiences, one that we say we live as a reality in life, and the other what we experience in our dreams and aspirations. When our dreams do not come true, we should not feel sad about it, but feel happy and privileged, that we were lucky enough to experience it in our dreams. To this I would again nod and say, "Hmmmmmmmmmm." He also told me that this was also called letting your life go with the flow, and not try shape your life the way you want it, but it take its own shape, its own course.

At times I would also get the inducing vibes and perceive great thoughts and say things like, "we all are born like blank canvases. And life keeps on spraying colours on us, red, yellow, blue, green, black. Which would make us feel angry, happy, sad, jealous, and evil or bad. To our like, or dislike, we keep getting sprayed by all these colours, and our life experience keeps getting richer. Till the day we die, making the painting called live, complete!' hmm, genius me, hmm, BOOM PRATEEK!

I say 'I love you' again.

"Raj, its high time you get a girlfriend! I have changed three boyfriends in the time you have taken to '*recover*' from the '*shock*' of you break-up with Hans!" Shilpa tried to convince me.

Shilpa and I had bunked the Building Construction class, as always (God! How boring it used to be!). We were sitting on the parapet in the corridor that we used to call the 'wind tunnel'. Its name had developed from 'high velocity winds' there owning to the narrowed down area of cross section of the corridor.

"It's not that easy yaar, I need a girl in order to make a girlfriend. And which three boyfriends have you changed?" I asked

"See, there was Abhishek, then Kunal, and then Dev. But that is not the point. You must get yourself a girlfriend." She said.

"What about Rushi? Why don't you propose to her?"

"???? What???? SHE SAID NO! Why the hell would I propose to her again??!!"

"See Raj, you have to see it the way I do – the great princess of *love*. Last time you proposed to her, you were …no one, you were in class X, had no idea where you are gonna be in the years to come." she said

"Ouch! That hurt!" I said

"I knew, it would, but that is the truth. Today, on the other hand, you are in one of the best architecture colleges in India, it's almost certain that you will be an architect after … if not four, then five or six years. That time you were a kid, now you are all grown up. See my point?"

I nodded.

I had been in constant touch with Rushi. I had never failed to wish her on *Holi*, *Diwali* or New Year on time. I always knew when her exams started, when they ended and when the results were to be out. I never failed to wish her best of luck, or congratulate her.

Shilpa was right. What was I waiting for? It was different then. I was grown up now. I was above 18! I was an adult, I could vote legally, get a driver's license and also open / operate my own bank account. (That is a different story that I didn't do / posses most of these things even today.)

"But she is not here? How would I meet her? I can't just get up and go to Jalandhar to see her you know! I have classes to attend!"

"So? Call her!" she said very matter of factly.

"No. That is what I did last time. And she said no. Phone is jinxed!"

"Ok. May be she can't take a decision if you put something right her face. Ok, write her a letter. E-mail. This is how the world runs these days. Write her a love e-mail."

So I sat down, sat down to write my first love e-mail.

Dear Rushi,

I have been in love with you ever since the first time we met. That time we were together all the time, so I never felt the need to ask for anything more. We grew up, took separate ways, I convinced my self that ... that was it, that was what was supposed to be, we were to meet, spent some time together in our childhood that we would remember and cherish throughout our lives. Then we met again. And had our share of precious moments together. When we were to drift apart again, I revealed my feelings to you; I told you that I wanted to spend my life with you. You said what if I like some one else? What if you like some one else? Well, today I am telling you. It has been three years and I have not liked 'someone else'.

I am telling you, I still like you. Still think about you as strongly as I did back then. Still can't think about anyone else. Still want to be with only you for the rest of my life. Still love. Yes, I love you. I still love you.

Waiting for your answer

Love,

Today and always.

Raj.

Dear Raj,

Its only when one loses someone, one realize his value. You were, you are and will always my most special friend. And what could be better than having your best friend as your companion for life. Back then we were young. ...I was unsure and... scared may be. But today I am sure. Yes. My answer is yes.

I always have, and still do, love you.

Yours,

Rushi.

This is what I wanted her reply to be. But what she had to say was,

Dear Raj,

O my God! I can't tell you how I felt when I got your letter. I like someone else.

Love

Rushi.

P.S – please try to understand, and please reply.

To this, I replied.

Hey!

That is so nice to know! ...Congrats! How is he? And who is he?!

Love,

Raj

To this she replied.

Dear Raj,

Thanx! He is my classmate. We were friends, almost from the day I joined college. Its only last month that things turned out this way. His name is Akash. He is also a Taurean. And by the way, I heard that you were going around with Neelhans. What happened?

Love,

Rushi.

To this I replied.

Hey!

That is nice to know! Hmm, so Akash haan? I would like to see what he looks like. Send me a picture of his. And as about Neelhans, Neelhans and I are NOT going around.

Love,

Raj.

To this she replied.

Dear Raj,

Hmm. So you want to see his picture haan? Don't worry, he is even skinnier than you, (you can beat him up. But don't worry, I know for a fact that he would never hurt me.) And please find a nice girl for yourself now (a nice girl who is better than me.) And don't worry; I am not hiding him from you. I am sending a picture of his. It's from our Goa college trip.

Love,

Rushi.

"Goa! They have been to Goa! Already! What is this! Have they already had their honeymoon?!" I was... I cant really express how I was feeling.

"Raj! Stop overreacting! They just went there on a college trip. She has very clearly specified that. As far as I know of your relationship, neither of you would lie to the other." Shilpa was...I guess trying to console me.

"...Ok! It was a college trip! But who can say what all happens on a college trip! I was telling you, form the very beginning, it was a bad idea to send her the letter." I complained.

"I just wish we had sent that letter a little earlier." She sighed.

"Huh! As if that would have made any difference?" or would it have?

I have a blast on my birthday.

PARTY TIME!

IT WAS MY BIRTHDAY! I had taken a day off from office and spent all day in the malls. Watching films! I finally saw *Tararumpum*! And felt extremely proud, when the kid sitting next to me said, pointing at Rani, "mom! This is the same aunty that fell down with that uncle and broke her ipod?"

With the smile of a saint I turned to that kid and told him "that aunty there my dear child, is Rani Mukherjee. And that uncle who she fell down with is Saif, Saif uncle." My God! What kind of mother did that kid have? Did she not care for her child at all??!! She was not teaching her even the basics! God! What is gonna become of this world! But anyways, after the movie, I had a very lavish lunch. Did some very lavish shopping – books, CDs, DVDs, clothes, everything! And Boom! It was party time! O MY GOD! It was 7:30 already! Was I late, were the guests there already? I reached my place as soon as possible. No one was waiting there. THANK GOD!

"SURPRISE!" everyone screamed as I opened the door.

"O my God! You guys are already here." I looked around. The whole place was decorated with fancy balloons and stuff. We had it all, it was a Disney theme party   Cars, Pirates of the Caribbean, Mickey, Minnie, Donald, Goofy, Beauty and the Beast, they were all over the balloons and the decorations.

Everyone was there, Guneet, Aksha, Shalini, Pragya, J.J, Raina, Deep, Manisha, Prateek, everyone! And yes, Prateek, that stupid idiot, he had come back early from office and let everyone in. He came and shook my hand. "Happy birthday," he said, and gave me a warm hug.

"Ok, ok, now my turn. Happy birthday." Guneet pushed him aside,

185

"happy birthday." She said, and handed me this kind of small-ish box, nicely packed.

"What! This is it! Such a small gift! That's it? Is this all that you are gonna give me?" I said, struggling to make my disappointment sound like a joke

"Shut up, and behave, you should be happy with whatever we give you. Gratitude. And this is not only from me; it's from all of us. Now open it."

ALL OF THEM! IT WAS A DISASTER! MY B'DAY WAS TURNING INTO A COMPLETE GIGANTIC TITANIC DISASTER!

I opened the present. IT WAS AN IPOD! "O MY GOD! O MY GOD, YOU GUYS!"

Guneet jumped with joy, "I told you he would like it! I told youuuu." It was her idea.

I was deeply touched. "Thank you guys." I turned to Guneet, "and thank you, for knowing what I was craving for secretly, thank you, you knowing me so well." I hugged her. And then we had a group hug.

"OK NOW, ENOUGH OF ALL THIS. LETS GO UPSTAIRS." Guneet said stepping back.

We went to the terrace. The weather was nice, soft cool breeze, soft moonlight.

"TIME TO CUT THE CAKE!" Guneet announced.

Ufff! Now what was that! I wanted a Black Forest cake. But nooooo! Who cares about what I want! But they got a fruit cake! Anyways, they got it, so, did not really matter; at least they got a cake. Gratitude!

A full set of 25 candles was set on the cake! And blowing them was *not* easy!

"Ok! Now cut the cake! Cut the cake!" Guneet wont stop jumping.

I cut the cake.

"I will feed him first! I will feed him first!" Guneet came towards me jumping.

SHE PICKED UP THE WHOLE CAKE AND **SMASH!** THE WHOLE CAKE WAS ON MY FACE!!!! And then there was a cake fight, just like we see in the old movies! Pieces of cake, from one corner to another! It was soo much fun! But poor Prateek looked so staggered! Anyways, after that Guneet got another cake, she was all splattered with the previous one, just like me. AND THE NEW CAKE WAS A BLACK FOREST CAKE!! We cut the new cake, in a very civilized manner. God! We all looked like savages that time!

After that we put on the music. Who so ever wanted to dance could dance and all. The rest of us were having coke or mountain dew, as per our choice, in the cups of our choice. We had quite a range car cups, poo bear cups, princess cups and pirate cups and many more.

I could see different people observing different people! Heh heh heh ! It was fun!

Raina was the first one to come and ask, "So, what is your friend Prateek's story? Does he have any girlfriend?"

"No." I said.

"Ok, so?" she said.

"So?" I asked.

"So? Would you go and introduce me to him??!!"

And so I did.

Raina and I went around serving chips.

"Prateek, have you met Raina?"

"No, actually I haven't." he said. A little hesitant

"Raina is a trainee working in my office. She is from Jaipur."

"Hi!" she made her move. "Where are you from?"

I left them alone, so that they could get to know each other better.

I went to a side and hardly must have taken two sips when Aksha came and asked me.

"So, J.J. is from Jaipur right?"

"Yes!" I said all excited "he is a very nice boy! I see a great deal of myself in him! You know, in office whenever I see him! He reminds me the way I used to be in office when I had just joined. He is very submissive. I keep trying to put sense into his head!"

Aksha was hardly listening to me. She was lost, dreaming away to glory. "Come, I will introduce him to you. I dragged a dreamy Aksha to a sad lost J.J. He had still not get over his break-up fully.

"Hi, you from Jaipur?"

I left them alone so that they could get to know each other more. They started talking to each other, sipping coke. Aksha from her Minnie Mouse cup, and J.J from his Mickey Mouse cup.

I was talking to Deep, "you know something, my best friend, back in 12th standard was a girl named Deep."

"Ok." Deep said, with interest.

"Isn't it a girl's name?" I asked.

"My full name is Deeptimay Ramamury. Deep is only a nick name." He explained.

"Hmmm." I nodded. It was then that I saw a very disappointed Raina coming to me.

"Yaar Raj, no use! He didn't show any interest. He didn't even ask for my number to exchange sms."

"What happened?" Deep asked.

"Yaar, that cute guy over there yaar. He is soo uff! I am sure he has a secret girlfriend!" Raina said with a frown and wrinkling her nose.

Hmm, may be they also needed to know each other more. So I left them alone.

> *I've been living with a shadow overhead,*
> *I've been sleeping with a cloud above my bed.*
> *I've been lonely for so long,*
> *Trapped in the past I just can't seem to move on.*
> *I've been hiding all my dreams and hopes away,*
> *Just in case I might just need then again some day*
> *all want to do is find my way back into love.*

The song was playing in the background. I could see that a lot was happening in the party. A LOT!

Office had become fun. Prateek had shown me the right path, and Pragya was showing me all the right attractions.

"I can see people, and I can see you." I looked directly into Pragya's eyes.

"What?" she asked all confused.

"What WHAT? Its from Titanic yaar, how can you not know?" I sounded a little frustrated. Pragya and I had started sitting next to each other in the office. And whenever we had a little free time we would talk, talk and talk. The boss had gone to Italy for a two-week tour. Office felt like a completely different place altogether.

"I have not seen *Titanic*." She said, all straight faced.

"WHAT!" she had uprooted my whole world! How could she have not seen *Titanic*! How come such a close friend of mine had not seen *Titanic*?! "Come on, how can that be? Even my dad had seen *Titanic*." I remembered how with great difficulty I had convinced him to got out and see the film in the cinema hall.

"Ya, seriously, I have not seen it. *Vakhaye, mai Hollywood ki filmay kum dehkti hoon you know.*" She said, imitating Preity from *Jhoom Barabar Jhoom*.

"You must be kidding!" I could not believe my ears.

Now how was I supposed to go on talking to her? What did she know about the world! What did she know about love!

"Raj. Would you please come here for a minute?" It was Shweta. She must have got work for me. Hmm, responsibility, she was gonna hand me over. I have never liked taking up responsibilities, not in life, not in office. Whenever anyone used to call to hand over any responsibility to me, I would always take great care to oil my hands well. So that when they hand me any work, it would slip out of my hands and I would go, "Ops! It slipped!" with a grin, from ear to ear.

I went to her.

"So, how are you today?"

O my god! Was she ok?!! Why was she talking to me like that?

"You must be thinking, I am always so mean to you. But Raj, I am just doing my job. I have to follow orders."

I kept looking at her. Should I have smiled, should I have I didn't really know.

"You and Pragya, really look cool together. Are you two going around?"

I ... don't know why, but I blushed.

"O god! Look at you! Now listen, all these plans are to be checked and sent to the landscape team and the hydrologist's team. TODAY! Now go and get back to work."

What was with her today? Maybe she *was* actually not that bad.

I went back to my seat. I could not wait to tell Pragya! "You know What, Shweta just asked me, she asked me if we two were going around!"

"Okay!" she said, raising her right eyebrow. "You know what! May be we should!"

"What!" was she out of her mind? We were just friends!

"Yes! Lets have a little fun with it! Lets tell people that we *are* going around!"

And so we did.

We were having tea in the evening. Such nice weather it was, cloudy, and a very gentle drizzle. The office complex, by the way has trees and plants everywhere. In the rains, it attracts a lot of peacocks as well. We were sitting there, holding the warm teacups, in the cool weather, sipping the steaming hot tea.

"So, are we going around?" I asked.

"I don't know. Are we?" she asked.

"I guess!" I replied.

"See, if we are, then please tell me, so that I can tell my boyfriend." She has a boyfriend, by the way.

J.J came and sat next to us with his cup of tea. "I don't know what is on with this office! It has gone all chaotic!"

"Why, what happened?" I asked. J.J was looking really hassled.

"I don't know! You two are going around! And inside! Deep and Raina Had an argument, and now, Raina is writing "sorry" on small pieces of papers and throwing them at Deep, and he is throwing them back at her."

Just then his phone started to ring. I knew who it was. (Aksha!).

"Hie!" he said and went to a corner to talk to her.

Hmm! Office, a completely different place in boss's absence.

Next day, after lunch, Pragya and I were washing our dishes. (In office every one had to wash ones own dishes after lunch. We were talking about how we find difficult to be mean to the people who are sad. And how I am generally very nice to people when they cry.

"*inhe ponch do Pushpa. I hate tears.*" I smiled and looked at her, imitating Rajesh Khanna. "It's just that I just can't stand tears." I said.

"So, if someone wants to you to be nice to them, he should

cry?" Pragya said, raising one eyebrow, looking at me.

I looked at her, and smiled, "Is that so? Do you really think so?' I asked. She responded, "Raj, you don't have to make everything so complicated! Some things are better left simple." We kept looking at each other, and the water from the tap kept running. Shweta came from behind and turned the tap off, giving me a friendly slap on the head. "Don't waste water!"

"What kind of guy wears red socks?" Pragya said, pointing at my favourite pair of socks the ones I was wearing that day. Then she smiled, "I know, a guy, WHO IS GAY!" she said and started laughing. That was too much. I was offended. I grabbed her by the arm and swung her around, just like Saif did in *Hum Tum*, after the song, *ladki kuon* and kissed her (don't freak out, kissed her on the cheek, not on the LIPS!')

"WOW! That kiss, it was too good for a gay guy!"

Ok, important lesson, for all the girls who are reading this never challenge a guy's sexuality. Never! Never do that. Unless you want him to do what I just did. It was Pragya so I kissed her on the cheek. If it were any other girl, I would have kissed exactly the way Saif had done in the movie.

"I generally don't like it when someone comes to meet me without flowers." She said. "And especially if that someone is one," she raised her eyebrow and looked at me, wiggling naughtily, "who says that he wants to be my boyfriend."

What was up? Where were we both heading?

Ha ha! Relax guys. We both knew. We were just having fun. Just some harmless friendly flirting and nothing more.

I win a Moscar Award for the best story of the year!

The third year of college. And we were having a blast! Guneet, Aksha, Shilpa, Shalini, Shweta and me, Whenever there was no class, we would hunt for an empty lecture room and have our Moscar ceremonies.

"AND THE MOSCAR GOES TO…" Shweta would scream. "SHILPAAA! For her wonderful performance in *Mikka Go*!"

"O MY GOD! This is… I can't believe it! O my god! Ok, first of all, mom and dad, this was not possible without your support…" she would tremble and shiver and speak and end her Moscar speech with tears. Every actress had to end her speech with tears. We were very much just friends.

"Thank you! Ladies and gentlemen, that was wonderful a performance by one of the greatest dances of our time, GUNEET, a big round of applause for her!"

"And now, for the best story," Shweta would continue, "may I call upon stage the best director in India ladies and gentlemen! Miss AKSHA!"

"And the Moscar goes to… yes! Raj! For his outstanding story for the movie *Horse on a House*!"

All the others sitting with us were to clap and cheer. Loud, so that it felt like an event.

☙

Shilpa and I would keep enacting the balcony scene from *Romeo and Juliet* in college. She would stand in the wind tunnel, which was on the first floor, and I would stand on the ground floor, below it. Shilpa standing there would pretend that she did not know I

195

was standing below, and say,

'O Raj, Raj! Wherefore art thou Raj.

Deny thy father and refuse thy name.

Or if thou wilt not, then I swear my love,

I will no longer be a Gavane'

It's but thy name that's my enemy,

And what is in a name, it is not hand nor foot nor arm nor face, nor any other part belonging to a man.

That which we call rose,

By any other name wont smell as sweet?'

After she would forget the dialogue and have no clue what to say next, I would come out and reveal myself to her sight,

'I take thee at thy word.

Call me but love, and I will change my name.

Henceforth I will never be Raj. I would be Rahul'

And we would keep going on, laughing, and breaking Mr. Shakes legs.

One day, Rushi called. (!!!!!)

"Hi!"

"Hey! O my god! What a pleasant surprise! How *are* you?!"

"I have never felt better." She replied. "And I have a very good news."

"You are coming to Gurgaon!" I said, wishing for the best.

"Yes."

"WHAT?" I could not believe my ears.

"YES!" she sounded very exited. "It's my training semester and I will be joining training in DELHI! Tarini telecom!"

"This is the greatest news I have got in a very long time!"

"Yes! I know!"

"AAAAAAAAAAAAAA" Shilpa screamed.

"AAAAAAAAAA" Guneet screamed.

"AAAAAAAAAAAA" Aksha screamed.

"Aa" Shalini screamed. (Well, almost.)

"O my god! You must make a move this time!" Shilpa said all exited!

Hmm, but there was a tiny complication. SHE LIKED SOMEONE ELSE!

Rushi and I were sitting in the Garden of Five Senses, on the rocky face near the amphitheater. The sky had those cotton like soft white clouds. The whole atmosphere was dappled with soft evening light and the last rays of sun were warm on my shoulders.

"So, how has it been, all these years?" I asked.

"Nice." She said. And then she told me all the stories of her college. Including the one in which she broke up with Akash. SHE HAD BROKEN UP WITH AKASH! But how could I have made a move while she was telling me about her break-up. It was very painful for her, and the last thing that I wanted to do that time was to hurt her more.

We sat there in silence for a while. Then I said.

"Do you still stare at the clouds and see animals, trees, fairies and landscapes in them?" I asked.

She smiled. "Yes."

"Look, there is a bunny, hopping away. And another one there, eating a carrot."

"Yes."

"And there, a wicked witch, flying on her broom, over that hill."

Next time we met at Priyas. She was wearing a long white dress looking like an angel. We were sitting in Barista, on the nice big couch, listening to the guitar playing in the background.

"So, how is your training going?" I asked.

"It's nice. It's just that they don't treat you like an …engineer. They look at you more like you like a peon."

"That is not nice." I said.

I wanted to ask her something. But I didn't know how to start. "So, seen any new movie?"

"No."

Silence.

"Rushi, I wanted to tell you something." I said, my heart thumping the loudest ever.

She looked at me.

"I still feel the same way about you. There, I said it. I feel like that. And I said that. Now what ever you say or do or think, does not make any difference. I had to say it, and I said it. Done."

She smiled and looked at me.

"*What*? Now at least say *something*! Its not easy saying it again and again you know!"

"Raj," she said smiling "I have just stepped out of a relationship. And I can't get into another one."

Yes, yes, I knew, she was saying no again. Uff! Why did I even try? After that we went to see *Harry Potter and the Prisoner of Azkaban*. Hmm. Interesting

I just didn't feel like going to office.

I woke up that morning and, just did not, feel like going to office. So I decided to call in sick. I do not lie. But you know what, it's OK to lie in ones professional life. The office rule was, according to boss, "Whenever anyone wants to take a day off, you can surely do. But you must tell Me." So, Italy or France, wherever boss may be, I must call him and tell him that I was sick and could not go to office that day.

"UHU UHU! Boss, this is Raj. UHU UHU!"

"Yes Raj, what happened?"

"Boss I am not very well, won't be able to go to office today."

"Ok, its ok Raj, Take care."

"Thanks boss."

"Bye Raj."

"Bye boss."

And there it was, a bright sunny, day, right in front of me! I was very happy. "Today I would smile at everyone. Blooming flowers everywhere!" I told myself.

Spiderman 3, that was the movie I decided to watch that day.

And so I went to see a film, dressed in my favorite yellow shirt, rusty brown jeans, and red shoes. DT City center, that is where I went to watch the movie. I was just about to enter the hall when my phone started to ring. The screen flashed

Boss Calling ...

HOLY SHIT! As always they had music playing in the

background, this time they were playing *Jhoom barabar jhoom*. And it was not playing at a low volume. I spun around in panic. THE FIRE ESCAPE! I ran towards it. Yes! The music was not that loud there. I received the call.

"Hi boss."

"Hi Raj, it took you long to receive the call. I was about to hang up. How are you feeling now? Since you have told me, I just cant stop thinking about you. What is that noise at the back?"

Bloody boss! I think God has made ticks and bosses for the same purpose – TO SUCK BLOOD! Why was it is soo difficult for him to have a relaxing holiday in a wonderful place like Italy! And was it not like super obvious that I was faking sick! Why was he all set to spoil *my* holiday?!

"I am feeling better boss, had come out to buy some medicines."

"Ok. Bye Raj."

"Bye boss."

I could not believe it! They had completely ruined it for Spiderman! They had had made a very crappy film! They had no right to do that. They had no right to ruin Spiderman like that! I mean like who would go to watch the next Spiderman movie! They had soo many things going on, but the film just wouldn't move! I kept sitting there thinking, ok, now that black insect thingy from outer space would do something, but it just wouldn't! And ditto the Sandman! A 2.5 hour movie felt longer than 3 hours! In the middle of the movie, the phone started to ring again. It was boss again. I did not receive the call. As soon as they showed the intermission sign on the screen, I got up and rushed to the fire escape again.

"Hi boss, you called?"

"Yes Raj, I was just wondering what actually is wrong with you?"

I had the whole story nicely put together already (obviously, who doesn't?) and the story was part true as well. As I have already told you our office had plants and trees of all varieties. And once I had become allergic to a specific kind of pollen. That time I was very frustrated and wondered why the hell did boss have to plant bloody all kinds of plants from the whole world his office compound. It would serve no other purpose but make sure that someone would grow allergic to some type of plant and then I don't know DIE MAYBE! But that time I took no day off. So it was completely fair to use the story.

"Boss I think I have become allergic to some plant in the office. That is what the doctor said."

"O My God! You should go to my doctors, these days most doctors don't know anything!"

Uff! You blood sucking ugly bat! GET OFF ME!

"No boss, my doctor is well qualified."

"Ok. Then we must find out which plant you are allergic to. We will kill it. What else can we do?"

Bloody #@$^ "kill the plant" yes, what else can he think, other than killing and destroying. Bloody plant killer. He should not have said that, knowing that I was such a true nature lover. But maybe he said that coz he knew that I was ... ok. So he was playing with me. Just then some youngsters came and sat next to me. Smoking and discussing the movie they were watching. Fire escape, it was the best place for smokers.

"What is that sound in the back Raj?"

"Nothing boss, I have not yet reached home."

"Ok, I thought I heard someone saying something about

Tararumpum." SHIT! RED ALERT! RED ALERT!

"Hello! Boss, I can't hear you. You voice is breaking up. Hello "

"Hello, Raj, can you hear me? Hello."

I disconnected the call. And called up Guneet immediately.

"Hello Guneet?"

"Hi chick..."

"Listen, can you hear the music in the background?"

"What music?"

"Any music?"

"No."

"Ok, thanks, bye!"

Thank God!

I spent the rest of the day in the malls. Looking at people around. There was this girl-boy couple. And the girl, O my God! She was walking hand in hand with her guy, wearing unimaginably sleazy clothes, as if she was saying, 'Look at me, ammmmm, we are soo much in looooove. We will hold each other's hands and keep walking together. Imagining each other together, without clothes! Ammmmm! We are sooo in loooove! Ammmmm! Bloody hotie!

There was another couple sitting at a table. They were discussing cricket. But looking at that @#% sitting there, one could easily tell that what she was thinking was ... look at me, I am all slick and chick like. I am asking my boyfriend how he likes the Indian cricket team, but actually I am wondering how he would look without his shirt. And how he would like me, without *my* top on? The guy kept staring at her exposed cleavage every now and then.

I went to the lift. A liftman was standing there.

"Ground floor." I said. He nodded.

The lift got stuck on the first floor. WOW! WONDERFUL!

But I had to do *something*. I got talking to the liftman.

"What is your name?" I asked.

"Ishwaak Tyagi." He was short, thin, dark and very unattractive to look at.

"And where are you from?"

"Bengal."

"How long are your duty hours?"

"Eight hours." He was answering all my questions as if I was some military commander and he my junior.

"EIGHT HOURS! Is that without any break?"

"Only one break."

GOOD GOD! And I thought my job sucked! Just then the lift started moving and the door opened. A giggling, laughing, short, sweet, curly haired Ishika was standing right in front of me. Wearing a long frock, with nice refreshing floral print (small flowers.) fresh as spring she looked. I stood there looking at her. Motionless.

A college affair.

Everyone around me seemed to have a girlfriend or a boyfriend. And this time, when Rushi had refused to accept my proposal, *again*, I decided, that I was gonna be open to the idea of making a girlfriend. I was twenty-one that time, and was not getting any younger. Shilpa had told me very matter of factly once, as she was eating fruits during lunch in college,

"According to Jane Austin, the chances of anything interesting happening in a girl's life after the age of 25 are around zero. And according to me, its not any different for men also."

(!!!!) That time, I freaked out, I had only four years in hand to find the girl I was to spend the rest of my life with. In college, the new batch of juniors came. And I was on a complete lookout for my girl. I entered the first year studio and looked around. I saw this small girl sitting huddled in a corner. Scared like a rabbit, which has seen a cat. I walked up to her.

"Hi! I am Raj"

"Hi."

"What's your name?"

"Ishika."

"Let's go to the canteen and have a coke Ishika." She could not have said no, I was her senior.

⌒

In no time we became good friends. Although we had no common tastes whatsoever, we would spend hours sitting together, talking

"Hi! I am Raj."

"Hi."

Silence

"And your name is?"

"Ishika"

to each other, on the phone, or when we met. We would go for movies together. "I don't like watching movies" she would say. She would generally fall asleep, on my shoulder. And I loved it. I would lightly kiss her on the head.

Very soon the whole college knew we were going around. It was really nice having a girlfriend.

☞

We kept standing there for a few seconds. Looking at each other. We had met after a very long time. The feel of her broom like hair (that was how I used to tease her back then.) came back to me as fresh as ever.

☞

One day, we were having one of those love talks.

"Raj, what did you like in me that you decided that I was the one for you?"

"Your broom like hair." I said, laughing

"Raj! Seriously, what made you fall for me?"

"Ya seriously, I was soo bowled over by broom like hair, and I could not resist. And I decided to accept you, with all your broomness."

She stared back at me.

"No, actually the innocence in your eyes, that is what made me fall for you."

"Ok, now you tell me, what made you fall in love with me?"

"That you were my senior."

"No, seriously." I laughed.

She had no answer.

⤳

"Hi." I said.

"Hi." She said.

"Came here alone?" I asked.

"Actually I have come to watch a film, these days I don't miss any. Will be waiting for a friend."

"Wanna have a coke in the meantime?"

'Ok.'

⤳

I had stayed at Ishika's place for the night. I had come for the evening and it got late and I decided to stay. She used to stay in a rented flat with two of her friends. It was morning and I was getting ready to go to college – having a bath. The bathroom door did not lock. It was understood that if you hear sounds from inside, you are not supposed to enter. I was shampooing my hair. And was having a little fun with it – I was trying different Wolverine hairstyles (Wolverine from X-men). Suddenly I saw the door open and saw Ishika standing there.

"AAAAAAAAAA!" I screamed.

"AAAAAAAAAA!" she screamed.

"WHAT ARE YOU DOING *INSIDE*?" I shout.

"Checking you out." She came closer. "I don't like very hairy men." She said pointing at me, moving her finger up and down.

☞

We went to the food court and sat there. There was a couple sitting next to us. A couple with a child. We had soo imagined us like them once ... two not-so-good-looking people, happy together, with a not-so-good-looking kid, content with their lives, and happy together. We sat there in silence, sipping our cokes.

☞

It was another night stay at her place. That day, after college I had gone straight to a men's parlour, and got myself waxed. And then I had gone to Ishika's place. I had the top three buttons of my shirt open. As soon as she saw me she noticed. "hmmm", she said, "neat." That night after dinner she put the radio on, the song was on '*pehla yeh pehla, pyar tera mera soni...*'

It was late in the night I was setting my bed on the floor to sleep. We both used to sleep in her room whenever I stayed over at her place. She used to sleep on the bed, and I used to put her extra mattress on the floor and sleep. "Raj, will you help me with this, I can't unhook this ...bra." She said, fumbling her hand under her top. "Can you help me with this?"

"Ya, sure!" Yeah baby! Yeah!

And then, off went her bra! That night we could not keep our hands off each other.

The kid who was with that couple came over and stood next to Ishika, and started staring at her. Children always used stare at her. Maybe they used to think "Hey! She is our age!" kids always used to get attracted to her. And at one point of time, I was also.

"Kids still come to you the way they used to do back then." I said.

Silence.

"O! She is here! My friend is here. It was nice meeting you. Bye." She walked away to her friend. I could hear her friend's voice fading as they walked away, "who was he? Was he the ..."

How did we break up? Well, after a point of time, I realized that the relationship was not heading anywhere and it was best to end it. The relationship was primarily based on our physical needs, and very little beyond that. Soon there came a time when we had nothing to talk about, and found each other happier talking to other people than talking to each other. Finally I decided to make the move, and I got all the blame. "I AM NOT A TEA CUP THAT YOU CAN JUST USE AND THROW AWAY RAJ!" she had accused me. But that was the best for both of us, the relationship was becoming a compromise, the quality of life had gone low. Back then I used to think about it a lot. And whenever I am on an emotional upheaval, I paint, to get them out, so that I can look at the paintings, and understand what I feel. I made another painting that time. I called it 'The Divorce.'

"Maybe they see something in her that normal people can't." Pragya said. I was telling Pragya About my meeting with Ishika the previous day. Maybe she was right, may be there was some inner beauty in her, that normal people could not see.

"Maybe something weird, that only children can see. Like some horns, or ... some aura over her head, which we *know* are there, but can't see." She said narrowing her eyes, acting like a female Sherlock Homes or something. "Or maybe they are just looking at her hair and wondering how to make a magical broom out of it and fly away."

"I still feel bad that I broke up with her. Poor girl, I broke her heart." I said, looking down at the floor.

"And why did you leave her?"

"I did not leave her. My love for her left me."

"Raj, I was in college all the time when you were going around. She was never in love with you. I never saw that in her eyes"

"Then why was she going around with me?" I asked.

"Because you were her senior. And it means something for the people around when a junior girl goes around with a senior in college, especially when the senior is some one like you." She said and started to walk away. I was even more confused now. 'But if she didn't love me then why did she create such a scene when I was leaving her?' I asked.

Without turning back, Pragya said, "Because she did not want to lose you."

The employees in the office win the battle for their rights.

Office! No matter how much you want, you can never get rid of it, unless,

your dad is a multimillionaire, and has loads and loads of property that you can make use of.

Or

Some stinkingly rich relative of yours leaves inexhaustible sums of money to your name when he dies.

Or

You win a lottery.

Or

You discover some magical tree on which money and other valuables like gold, diamonds and pears grow. (Everyone's ultimate fantasy!)

But it was not that bad that day. Boss was not around. So no sitar sounds for a while. That day, I got off happily at the red light, walked to the fruit vendor, bought my everyday portion of three bananas and happily walked to office.

I sat down and turned my computer on. Manisha came in, "Hi Raj! How are you?"

"I am fine. How are you?"

"I am fine, is it true what I hear?" she asked.

I smiled; I knew what she was talking about. "What?" I still asked.

"You and Pragya. Are you two going around?"

I laughed. "No! Not at all, she already has a boy friend, we just thought of having a little fun out of it, by spreading the rumour." I said.

"Well, she is waiting for you outside in the garden."

"Ok", I said

I got up and saw Shweta coming. I sat down again.

"Hi Raj." She said.

"Hi Shweta." I said.

"Raaahul! You don't have to go back to your seat if you see me coming. Go, Pragya is waiting for you outside."

Hmm, everyone had started to believe the joke. Hmmmm.

That day, 10th of May 2007, Delhi Government had declared a public holiday. The 150th anniversary of India's first freedom struggle. AND WE WERE ALL WORKING THAT DAY! And we were not ok with it. Who has not seen *Rang de Basanti.* We decided to rebel. When we asked for the rest of the day off (which was slightly impractical.) we were told, 'that can not happen. And from this week on, there would be no second Saturdays off.' We were outraged! To this, we all decided to express our discontent. Pragya was the first one to speak up. She went to G2three2 and said, "G2three2, we have no life at all. Its like we have sold our lives to this firm."

G2three2 replied, "No, that is not true, this is not the case."

She looked into his eyes, fuming. "It is true G2three 2, we never get any national or gazetted holidays, most of us were working on *Holi*, some people were even working on 26th Jan, and now even the second Saturdays have also been declared as working. It is really like we have sold our life to this firm."

"O come on, that is ridiculous, you know that is not true." He replied, laughing, "you are overreacting."

She glared at him, angrier than before. "In that case", she said, "I quit."

Hearing this G2three2 peed in his pants (almost).

"No, no. Ok, call every one else, lets have an open meeting, it seems people are very discontented out here."

And so, everyone was called.

A two hour long discussion followed. During which, we all expressed our extreme disgruntlement about long working hours and no day off. We all said, "The reporting time is there, but the leaving time is not fixed."

At this, we all were attacked individually, I was told, "Raj, your output and productivity has gone down like anything in the last few months." He (G2three2) turned around and looked at Pragya, looked back at me and went on, "you really worked very hard and seemed very clear-headed when you joined. But now, you have lost all of it, it's hit rock bottom."

IMAGINE, HE SAID THAT, IN MY FACE, IN FRONT OF EVERYONE.

"So, there has to be a reason for that, right?" I said.

"Yes, tell us." he replied.

"As has just been pointed out, it's the way the office works. The system is so tight, we don't even get time to breathe!"

"Raj in the whole office, you should be the last one saying this, I think you are the one who gets the maximum time to breathe."

This was too much now; it was like calling me out for a duel! Manisha caught my expression, she knew I was gonna blow my top, she intervened. "But G2three2, all we are asking here for one day off in the whole month that is not Sunday. So that we can all relax for a while and do all the work that cannot be done on a Sunday, like paying the bill and all."

As she was saying this, I could here footsteps from behind. Accompanied by background music from *Star Wars*, Dum Dum Dum Da Dha Dum Da Dha Dum! It was Ajeesh Kuvakadan   the man in charge of the office in the boss's absence. God! That time! He looked soo much like Darth Vedar!

"Second Saturdays will not be off from now on." he turned and looked at us, his eyes, my God! It was as if he had some supernatural power, by which he could suffocate people merely by looking at them, I ...could not ... breathe! He turned his gaze away, huff! The invisible hand released my neck, uhh! I could breathe again. Then he went on, saying "and I know as a fact that coming and leaving on time, can not increase the productivity of the office. And you, Manisha, we did not expect you to put forward such demands, being a senior architect. However, looking at the present scene, this Saturday will be off. The meeting is dismissed." He went out. The meeting was over.

"Is there any problem?" Neelam, did I ever tell you about her, well if I haven't its good, coz who wants to know the wicked witch of the north? (I call her this coz she sits in the north-facing wall of the office.) She is this female working in the office and is *very* career oriented. Boss takes very little decisions without consulting her. She was senior to Manisha in college.

"No." G2three2 replied, "all has been taken care of."

"Good. Or I would have taken care of It." she said, looking Pragya and me from head to toe, and then she left.

After everyone dispersed, Manisha came to me and said, see, its not that bad an office, it does a lot for you, you just have to say things politically right, the office does care for you and understand your needs.'

That day I left office very disturbed. I went to CCD and ordered for my daily dose of Strawberry Iced tea with honey.

"What happened sir, you look very upset." Santosh said, as he placed my drink on the table.

"Nothing really, its just office." I said.

"I think you should take a break sir."

"He does talk sense" I thought, "I should go out this weekend! Macleodgunj! It is an overnight journey by bus. A weekend's was perfect for the trip!"

YES! THAT WEEKEND! I WAS OFF!

Me and Shilpa become Bunty and Bubbly and cheat a hotel and get big fun out of it.

Hmm! The fresh air and the magnificent beauty of the mountains! It was too good to be true! Misty clouds floated lazily around the mountaintops. The deodar trees seemed to do their own little dance with the wind, slowing swaying from side to side. Hmmm, it was beautiful, actually, beautiful is an understatement, it was splendid!

I had come to this place before. 1.5 years back, after I was through with Ishika. When Shilpa and I had decided that we were gonna work in the mountains.

"I have it all planned out", she had said then, "there are two architects in the region, we will join the bigger office out of the two, and then, slowly, slowly slowly and slowly, we will TAKE OVER THE OFFICE! And then we can live here! Forever and ever!"

⌒

We entered the hotel room, "My god! This is just not done!" an offended Shilpa exclaimed, "This is not even funny!"

"Ya", I agreed, "they can't charge us fifteen hundred bucks per night for *this* filthy room!"

"Don't worry, we are not gonna pay him." She said flatly.

"But how?" I asked.

"Just wait and see." She said looking around the room, narrowing her eyes.

⌒

I was walking on the streets of Macleodgunj. I reached the main

216

square, the bus stand area. Memories of Shilpa were still fresh. We had spent so much of time there together. I felt her presence everywhere. I saw the bench on the edge of the road, where we had sat for hours, making fun of the foreign tourists around, imitating their accents. I went and ran my hand gently on the armrest of the bench. It transmitted a smile to my face. I sat down and closed my eyes.

"I have heard that there are a lot of food snatching, face scratching monkeys in the area." Shilpa said as she munched chips that we had bought a few minutes ago.

"Yes", I said, with my nose in the thick paperback edition of *Lonely Planet.* "Hey look at that, that guy in the red t-shirt, with brown coloured ropes instead of hair! God! Does he not look funny?! Look at him going, exkhuse me sa. Which way is the temple sa?" she said, "O! And look at that! That fat blonde! My god! What did she eat! And look at the… AAAAAAAAAA"

I looked up and saw, a monkey was running away with her packet of chips.

"UKH! Stupid monkey!" She said, "anyway, hey look at that…"

After a few minutes I opened my eyes, and got up. I took the road that went up the hill, to the German Bakery.

"And you know what?" Shilpa said sipping fresh watermelon juice that she had ordered from the German Bakery, "after we establish ourselves as architects, we can also have our own restaurant. There, we can offer that special rose drink that my mom tells me is very good for the heart." Shilpa told me as I was struggling to finish the pasta I had ordered, it did not taste very good. I was getting a little irritated with the pasta, so I said, "you know what is not good for health? THIS PASTA." We finished our food, got up and started walking down the road that took us to the hotel. We were walking, enjoying the beauty around. Shilpa had a bottle of coke in her hands that she was happily sipping and enjoying the beauty around. The sky was overcast with clouds. There was something that made us feel that we were in a forest in some fairytale land. The wind felt cold against the skin. Suddenly I heard Shilpa scream again! 'AAAAAAAAAAA' I turned around in alarm to see what had happened. A monkey was running away with her coke bottle.

We were on our way back to the hotel when it started to rain. Both of us opened our big multicoloured umbrellas and continued walking. After a while I realized that Shilpa was not walking next to me, I turned around and looked. She was standing on the edge of the road, looking at the valley. The air was foggy. There was a very faint layer of mist through which I could see her big multicoloured umbrella. I went next to her and stood there for a good five minutes. The view was very beautiful, a small stream ran through the centre of the valley and there was a rocky stretch on either side, beyond that there were dense woods. The thin clouds hung lightly over the valley. It was spellbinding. Almost magically, it brought a smile to my face. After some time, I touched her on the shoulder; she turned and looked at me. She had tears in her eyes. Wiping them she smiled, and said, "its very beautiful Raj." I hugged her, and we walked back to the hotel, hand in hand.

We were sitting in our hotel room. All set to go back. We were through with our groundwork and research, to take over a local office in the area, the task for which we had come on this trip.

"But how are we gonna escape from this hotel without paying?" I asked all frowned and worried.

'Very simple, we are gonna do the 'Bunty and Babli' trick." She said, drawing a heart on the mirror and writing S and R in it, with her lipstick. 'See we don't have much luggage with us, just our two small bags. So we are gonna leave the hotel, with our bags on our back. And if anyone asks, we are gonna tell them that we will be back in the evening, and we are just going out." She said, with naughtiness twinkling in her eyes. " And, we are gonna leave this letter behind."

The letter read,

Dear Maharaja Hotel,

Thank you so much for this most wonderful stay. We thoroughly enjoyed the company of the big fat rat in our room during the night. It was very thrilling. The mischievous thing kept making funny noises from all the different corners of the room and kept us well occupied all night.

The sounds from the steamer right outside the window made us believe that we were next to a huge, turbulent and magnificent waterfall.

The marvellous reflection of the snow covered mountains right across the valley, on the glass pane of the window, which could not be moved beyond an angle of 45 degrees, has given us tremendous new and creative ideas as architect.

The view of the high wall of the adjoining hotel, which killed all the possibilities of any kind of sunlight entering the room, was also very intimidating. The green moss patterns on the same wall were also very inspiring for us as designers.

The wonderful patterns of dampness in the room and the toilet roof were of utmost beauty.

It was really exiting to see the W.C. without a seat and the condom stuck in the drain.

The fear of the ablution tap or the flush not working, while we were shitting must have helped me reduce some weight for sure.

Thank you for the most unique stay at your hotel.

Love and Kisses (with pink roses)

Shilpa and Raj

After I came back from that trip with Shilpa, I went on another trip, a dream trip where I had opened an office with Shilpa, in the mountains, and we had got married and our children were playing in the beautiful garden, that we had landscaped together, in the Japanese style. But those dreams were soon shattered. One day she came and told me, "Raj, I am going to Africa."

!!!!!! WHAT!!! WHEN? WHERE? HOW?!!!!

"How come all of a sudden? You never told me before." I asked.

"Even I didn't know Raj. But my dad is getting posted to Angola, to develop the railways there, and my mom, and I are to go with him. I have no idea what I am gonna do there." She paused for a few seconds, and then she said with a frown, "May be I will teach the hungry, poor and naked kids."

And she was gone. This led me to make another painting. I called it 'The Departure'.

I feel that cell phones are a menace, and then I feel they are a necessity.

I reached home late in the evening. It was Sunday, Prateek had been home all day. He was sitting in front of his laptop, working on it soo engrossed that it seemed as if he was gonna get whisked into the screen any moment. When he saw me, he said, "*Haanji* sssir! How was your trip?"

"Pretty good actually, very relaxing. But the long bus journey was really something! It was like fourteen hours, in the bus."

"You must be very tired, I will order food at home."

"Thanks!"

"My pleasure."

I went to my room, had a bath and changed. Its killing I tell you, when you come from a nice cool hill station, to a place as hot as hell! Gurgaon summers I tell you!

I sat on my bed, resting my back against the wall, closed my eyes and relaxed.

My phone started to ring. MY GOD! These cell phones I tell you! They are a curse to mankind. No matter how much you may want to relax! These stupid tiny boxes just won't let you. Who the hell on earth was calling me? I looked at my phone, an unknown number! Wonderful!

"Hello." I received the call.

"Hello, Raj?" a somewhat familiar voice said.

"Raj! Haaaaaiee! How are you!" O MY GOD! IT WAS DEEP, MY SCHOOL FRIEND DEEP!!! AFTER ALL THESE YEARS! (May be cell phones were not that big a curse after all!) I was soo thrilled to hear her voice after six long years.

"DEEP! Hi! How are you! My god! I can't believe this! Wow!"

"I am fine. How have *you* been Mr. Architect?"

"Wonderful, right now I would say, never felt better! Where are you these days? And where did you get my number?' I asked, getting my senses back.

"I am in Jalandhar these days, and got you number from your mom you idiot! Where else would I get it from? And guess what! I am getting married!"

"WHAT! O MY GOD! WHAT!" What was she saying? Was this an age to get married?! We were only 25! May be it *was* our age to get married! Being most overly optimistic about our life span, we would live to be a hundred years. And even if we went according to that, we were through with 1/4th of our life, and had only three parts left in our hands! Shit!

"Where did you meet him! *How* did you meet him! Arranged or love?" I had soo many questions; I didn't even know where to start.

"Love marriage, he was with me in college."

Suddenly I experienced a huge sense of loss. She had found her partner and was getting married, and I didn't even get to know when all that happened! She had been my best friend, and I wasn't there with her, to share her feelings, when she was taking the biggest decision of her life. I felt I had lost out on something big. Working hard in college all these years, cutting myself off completely from the whole world for all this time, and then, after that, taking up a job that didn't even give me time to look at myself in the mirror, I had even forgotten what my hands looked like. It was not a nice feeling.

"He is from Chandigarh."

"Ok." I said, looking at my hands. Remembering how back in school everyone used to tease me for the way my hands looked,

222

slender, long fingers, pink delicate skin. "You have hand like girls." Ritesh used to come and say, suddenly everyone from my childhood came to visit my memory, Pragati, Vani, Mona, Rushi, Neelhans, Mrs Rai, Mrs Bajwa, my math teacher,. And all the time spent with them seemed to be far back in time.

"Raj, What happened? Where are you lost? I have not called you to listen to your silence after all these years."

"Sorry. Ya! So."

"So what? Any girl in your life or you are still stuck with Rushi?"

"Me, ya, no, actually no girls as yet."

'Hmm, I see.'

Was she right? Was I stuck with Rushi? Was that what I was up to all these years? Struggling to get over the idea that I cannot end up being together with Rushi, and failing successively?

"So", she went on, "have you put on some weight or are you still that thin?"

"I guess I am still that thin."

"I have put on quite a lot! Thank god I made a boyfriend before I put on weight! These days all the boys just run away like cockroaches as soon as they spot me!"

I smiled. She was still as funny as ever.

"How are Karan and Ashima?" I asked, I still remembered her cousins very vividly.

"They are fine, very good actually, Ashima is in 12th and Karan is in 10th. Now they are of the age that we were, when we first met." When Deep said that, nostalgia of the strongest order hit me. The images of Hans, came back all soo fresh. Our Maths teacher Iota, Megha, the girl, that vamp! The young girls and boys. I could see Neelhans's shy smiling face once again. I missed her more than I had ever missed her all these years.

"And they are in the same school now." She said. Those kids! They used to play cops and robbers back in those days. Young Ashima and Karan, running after one another, with toy pistols in their hands, screaming, 'I want to be police!' 'NO! I want to be police!' They had grown up soo big! It was very hard to conceive!

"So how have you been all these years? I want to know everything." I said.

"Ya, I know, after school ended, I joined college, and then ..."

⌐

I had my favorite *Dal Makhni* and *Roti* that Prateek had ordered and went to my room to sleep. The phone started to ring again. NOW WHAT! Who the @#$%^& hell is calling me now! I picked my phone, the screen was flashing,

Rushi Calling ...

O! It was Rushi! Ok!

"Hey! Hi!" I said

"Hi! Guess what? I have good news!" she said

"YOU ARE COMING TO GURGAON!" I exclaimed.

"YESS!"

"O my God! When?"

"Day after tomorrow!"

"Wow! What time?" I asked all excited.

"Actually I am coming there for an official meeting. Will get free at 5 O'clock in the evening. The meeting is in a hotel, Park Plaza. And I will leave for the air port at 6."

"Ok, we have one hour, to spend together."

"Yes." She said

"Ok. Cool. And what else?" I asked.

'Nothing yaar, getting a little sick of life now. I want to settle down. With someone, in a nice quiet place, peacefully.' She said.

O my God! What was she saying! Was she trying to tell me that that time I wanted to say, Come, come live with me that is what I wanted to tell her that time. I will take you there; I will take care of you, forever. I will always keep you happy. We will live in a small house, in the mountains, will have a cute little Apso dog, a huge garden, full of flowers and trees. But I did not. I did not say anything. And that is when it struck me. Deep was right! I had been stuck with Rushi. For all these years, struggling to get over the idea that I cannot end up being together with her, and failing successively.

I feel suffocated.

I woke up the next morning happier. All refreshed! That mini break had really worked! I had never felt better. I was walking to my office with springing steps! I loved the ten minute walk, loving it all   buying the three bananas. The fruit seller also knew me now. He greeted me very nicely. '*Namaste* sir, *yeh leejiay aap ke teen kelay.*' What did he really mean, well I didn't really care, he was talking nicely. I went on walking, eating the bananas. After I finished the bananas, I fed the skins to the cows, which, like everyday, seemed to appear magically as soon as I would finish my bananas. I went on, doing the weird tribal dance, (the bamboo jumping dance) over the fresh cow dung cakes lying all over the road, avoiding to step on them and listening to the songs on my lovely new ipod.

I reached office and boss's car was already there. God! He was back! But anyways, he was to come back, someday, so it was ok. Boss came up to me and said, "Hi Raj! How are you feeling now?" how was I feeling! Fine! What was wrong with me? O! The allergy! O yes!

"I am better now boss." I replied, coughing, trying looking a little sick. Thank God I had not shaved for the last three days! It really helped the look.

"Ok, now you can get back to work, as there is a *lot* of work, and we *really* need to work hard." Yes yes! As if I didn't know that.

A few minutes later Pragya came and settled down. It was so nice sitting next to her; we had complete access to as much chatting as we wished to. But she looked a little cross today. "Hi Pragya." I said.

"Hi, I don't know what G2three2's problem is. Ram, the office boy didn't deliver the documents to the people he was supposed to. And it's my fault! This is really sick! We are blamed for all the things that we do, and all the things that we don't do! This is not nice! Uh! Anyway. So tell me how your trip was."

Just then Manisha came from behind and said, "Hi everyone. I am leaving and came to say good bye to you all."

WHAT!

"WHAT! WHY? I MEAN WHY ARE YOU LEAVING?" it was not right, I must be hearing it wrong!

"To that I would just say that I am not leaving by my own will. I have been asked to leave." Saying that she turned around and started to walk away.

"But how come all of a sudden?" I said.

She had reached the door and opened it to go out. She turned around and holding the door she said, "because I guess that is the price one has to pay for speaking up."

"But that is not fair! If anyone had to get fired for speaking up, it should have been me! Or Pragya maybe!"

"May be you were lucky. Or may be not." She looked at me and saw me looking sad. She was leaving. I was gonna lose touch with her! How was I to meet her again! Or talk to her again!

"Raj," she said, "I may be leaving this office, but I am not leaving behind the friends that I made here. They will always be very dear to me." She smiled. Her lovely smile, I saw it again. But it scared me, was it the last time I was gonna see that smile. I struggled to force a smile. She smiled back and left. Pragya, J.J, Deep, Raina, me, we all were left sitting in our chairs, stoned.

After that meeting day, Ajeesh had called up boss. He told boss that there was a major upheaval in office. And that Manisha had gathered the whole of the young staff in office and put forward her demands in front of him and G2three2.

Ajeesh had never liked Manisha. He always wanted her out of the office. Listening to this boss was very furious. And he did not support Ajeesh for giving that Saturday off. "We bloody pay them. And they keep asking for holidays, why did you give in?" he demanded. To this Ajeesh replied that Manisha had left him with no option. He had got a golden chance to get her out of the office; he wouldn't let it go.

After that boss called up Neelam, "what should I do Neelam? What she did is not acceptable." He had asked her. Neelam was from the same college as Manisha was. Manisha was a year junior to her. But by far better looking and a better student. Manisha had won a gold medal from her college that was considered the best architecture college in India. Throughout college everyone liked Manisha better than her, in office the entire younger staff liked her better. She was also a major threat to her position in office also. "Boss, sack her." She said.

When G2three2 was asked he could not have told that it was he who called for the open meeting, or his job would have been in danger. "Boss I think we should sack her." He had also said.

Boss called Manisha on Sunday morning, and asked her not to come to office anymore. It would be better if she started looking for a new job for herself. She insisted that she should be told the reason why she was being asked to leave as that was her right.

To this she was told that she was being fired as she had not been able to give any deliverables in the past two months, and that she was politicizing the office and poisoning people's minds.

The whole office was shaken up. No one was being able to work.

Everyone was sitting in their seats and zooming in and zooming out on cad on their computer screens. I was not even able to do that. I just kept sitting there, sitting, staring at my computer screen.

~

'It's getting very warm.' Raina said.

"We should turn the AC on." I said.

I got up and turned the AC on. And I started closing the windows, one by one. And as I went on closing the windows, I felt the suffocation in the office building, with each window closing. I just wanted to run away from that place.

~

It was lunchtime. Everyday, this used to be the time to celebrate the break. Someone or the other out of J.J, Deep, Raina, Pragya or me would get up all excited and pull every one out of their chairs and drag them out for lunch. "Lunch time people! All the computers off please." We would say. I remember actually lifting Deep up one day, putting him on my shoulder and taking him out to the café.

I got up and said, "Lunch time people." But my words did not bring any change in the gloominess that was hanging in the air in the room. I got up and went to the door. I pushed the door open; it felt heavy, heavier than it had ever felt before.

~

We had had our lunch. We were sitting there, on the bench, with our empty plates in our hands. 'When I joined this office, there was a party that evening. We had a bonfire right there.' Pragya said, pointing at the spot where we always used to have bonfires in the office in winters. 'That time, everything looked so fresh. Now it looks all so stale.'

With the empty plate in her hand she stretched her arm out, "Imagine", she said, "If a pound of good luck comes and falls on this plate from the sky."

"May be it has, it has fallen on the plate." I said.

"That is what, maybe it has fallen already, may be I have eaten it." she paused for a few seconds, and then said, "Or maybe I will end washing it off."

We both got up and went to the café, to wash our plates.

I was asked to go to the store on the top floor and get some tile samples. I went there. It was a dingy little room with only one beam of light touching the floor, coming in from a high window. There were cobwebs on all the boxes in the room. Things had been this way since a long time there. No one had ever tried to do anything to bring about any change in that room – to make it better, to improve the way things had been stacked in the most unorganized manner. Everything seemed trapped, bound against it's will, tied! There was a small piece of cello tape on one of the old boxes lying there. The tape was half stuck on the box and half fluttering with the wind, as if wanted to be set free and fly away. I did not like it; I wanted to set it free. I pulled it off the surface of the box and released it. It went flying away with the air. It looked happy, I felt happy. That is when I took the decision. I was going to quit.

People ask me the same weird question over and over again.

I was sitting with Pragya in the food court of Mega Mall after office. I was wearing a black t-shirt that said 'To be or not to be, that is the question.'

"I am gonna tell boss tomorrow that I will quit." I said

"So, you have made up your mind." She said.

"Yes." I said

"Good. I am gonna miss you. A lot. Its gonna be tough, being in that office now, without you by my side."

I looked at her and smiled. "Don't worry, I know you are strong enough."

She looked at me and smiled, "Thanks, and so are you, taking such a decision is not easy."

I smiled back at her. "Are you gonna tell boss why you are leaving?" she asked.

"Yes."

"Good. You should. Otherwise there is no point." She said

There was silence for a few seconds.

"Guess what!" I said trying to make the atmosphere a little light, "Rushi is coming to Gurgaon tomorrow!"

"Okay! And are you gonna propose to her this time?"

" Why would I do that? I mean why??"

"I don't know, maybe because you always do, whenever you get the slightest chance."

I smiled, and asked, "Do you think I should?"

"Well! She *is* one of the reasons that we are not going around! I can't think of any reason why you should not!"

Later that evening I was to meet Shalini at the mall.

"Rushi is coning to Gurgaon tomorrow."

"Ok, so are you gonna propose to her?" she said

"O god! Why does everyone keep asking me that!" I said, slightly irritated.

She smiled and looked at me, "You should know the reason. Ok tell me, why did you not accept Aksha as you partner?"

"Coz I didn't feel about her that way." I said, very simply.

"And why was that?" she asked.

I thought for a minute. "Coz I was getting over my old relationship with Ishika."

She gave me hard look, "Really?" she asked.

"No, coz I had always got my heart set on Rushi." I said very meekly.

That evening when I was having dinner with Prateek, I told him too. And he said,

"So, are you gonna tell her the way you feel about her?"

"NO! AND WHY WOULD I DO THAT!"

"Sorry! I just thought that " he fell silent.

"What?" I asked.

"I just feel that a nice guy like you ...should be with a nice girl like her. You keep writing things like these down in that red notebook of yours."

"How do you know that? And when did you read it?" I asked sounding a little offended.

"I never read it. You only told me about it once. When you told me about Rushi. I have not read It." he looked a little scared.

"O! Ok. So you think I should propose to her tomorrow?"

"Yes."

"I don't think so. I have done that thrice already."

Yes, it did not make any sense. I don't know why everyone around me had gone completely and utterly MAD!

"But those three proposals didn't change your relationship with her. I don't think a fourth proposal would, in anyway, change your relation with her... for the worse"

Hmm. Really?

I hold my head up high, and tell my boss in his face that HE SUCKS!

I woke up next day and got ready for office. Completely aware of the fact that today was going to be my last day in office. It was my last walk in those tight streets of the 'urban village'.

I reached office, turned on my computer and waited till everyone came. Everyone seemed to be in a bad mood already. J.J, Raina and Deep entered frowning. "Why the hell is it soo hot in Delhi, and the buses have to be soo overcrowded!" J.J complained. Pragya came and sat next to me, "So, today is *the* day."

"Yes." I said.

"What is going on here?" Raina asked.

"I am leaving this office." I announced.

"*Yeh lo!*" J.J said, crashing in his chair.

'Why Raj?' Deep asked softly.

"What has happened is not right. And someone has to take a stand and raise a voice against it. I have decided that I will do it today." Pragya smiled and looked at me.

"Cant you stay on for a little longer Raj. Till our training gets over, for another fifteen days." Raina said.

"Boss needs to be answered back. Today. Not after fifteen days." I said.

Shweta entered the studio. "Hi Raj!" she said.

"Hi Shweta." I replied. She was walking towards her seat. She looked at me and stopped. "What is wrong?" she asked.

"I am quitting today."

"What! Shut-up! moron! Stupid jokes early in the morning! Sit down and get to work."

I did not move. She looked at me for a few seconds. "You have decided."

"Yes."

"And your decision is final."

"Yes."

"Ok. Ok. It was nice having you around."

Silence.

Just then Boss walked in. All the sitar sounds on earth following him.

"Hi, Deep, hi Raina, hi Raj, hi Pragya, hi J.J" he said while he was walking past everyone.

"Boss I have something to tell you." He froze, and turned around. All the sitar sounds ceased – complete silence

"What is it Raj?" he asked in a very sympathetic voice.

"Boss, I will not be working in this office today onwards."

"Why Raj, what happened.' He had not seen it coming. One of the greatest architects in India did not see a puny, meek employee of his, quitting, and walking out of his wonderfully magical kingdom.

"Boss I have lost faith in this office and I can't work here anymore." I said. I had never been more serious, in my life.

"Why is that Raj?"

"Because of the things that have been happening in this office lately."

"What in particular?"

"The way Manisha was fired."

"Ok, in that case I would like to tell you why I had to sack her."

"Boss I am not questioning you for what you did, and why you did so, but it's the way ..."

"No, you must know both the sides of the story."

He had started. I knew he would go on now. I kept quiet. "She had not been able to deliver any deliverables in the past two months. Before that she was sick for one month, she had *paid* leave. She took a lot of days off. No work happening. As a boss I had done a lot for her. And after that, in my absence she makes a puny gang of these innocent young people in the office and puts forward *her* demands. When after ten years I have gone away on a holiday, she politicizes the office and poisons people's mind. I can't accept that. Is that how one is supposed to pay back."

"First of all Boss, I would like to say that I did not ask you why you fired her."

"Ok, I thought you wanted to know why she was fired."

"No Boss, that is not the case, it's your office and you have the right to run it the way you want to. Secondly, it's not who was fired, and why that person was fired. It's how that person was fired. One can not call up an employee and ask him to stop coming to office the next day onwards. Thirdly, I have been a part of this office long enough now and I know how hard working she was. And even if she could not deliver, she should have been warned in advance and given notice. Fourthly, it is an office policy that has been laid down and one can not classify it as a favour, giving paid leaves that is, so no question of gratitude. As to about politicizing the office and poisoning people's minds, Manisha had always been the one who would hold people back whenever there were chances of an upheaval in the office, she would always ask people not to disturb you as the office worked at many transparent layers for the well being of the employees and boss should not be disturbed as he had so many other tensions and things to take care of."

I could see tiny droplets of sweat on Boss's forehead. He got up, took a step or two towards the door and came back. Again he started, "If you are basing your decision on this one incident, I don't really respect it. But I must tell you that other offices have military rule. You have to report at a fixed time and leave at a fixed time." I looked at him and smiled. He gave me a blank look and continued, "we are a very open and flexible office, it will be very tough for you to go and adjust anywhere else. We live like a family here. We care for you. I care for you."

I looked at him again and smiled. "Boss, I don't want to be a part of a family in which you get thrown out because you have been ill."

He stood up, took a few steps towards to the door and came back. "People who have been able to adjust to the work culture of this office have reached places like, Boston and Berckley. One can go places, if one adjusts here. Even now, after all that you have said, if you decide to stay, I am ready to take you back. I am not asking for an answer right now. You can take your time, decide, and tell me." he got up and left.

None of his weapons had worked, he tried to make himself look like the guy who was very kind and did a lot for everyone and never got paid back, it did not work, he could not win my sympathy.

He tried to scare me; it didn't work.

He tried to attract; it didn't work.

I supported the truth. I refused to kill my conscience and keep climbing the ladder, or keep walking on the road to 'success'. I refused to lose my integrity. I didn't really know where it would lead me, probably nowhere. But I knew one thing, if I would have walked on, on that road, it would have led to a living hell.

Half and hour after the Boss's speech, I went to boss. I opened the studio door, it did not feel as heavy as it had the previous day. I told him that today was my last day in office and I would be leaving after lunch, as I had to meet someone.

What is the first thing that one is supposed to do when one quits one's job, or loses one's job because of any reason? START PLANNING A HOLIDAY! Or actually may be not, may be, one is supposed to go back home ... go back home, watch *Black* for another time and cry one's eyes out. And *then* start wo.king on planning the holiday!

I stepped into my room and had a look around. It was in a great mess. Heaps of clothes everywhere. Empty packets of potato chips make crackling sounds as I stepped. Empty bottles of Coke and Pepsi rattled away as moved carving my path forward. It had been almost a year since I had cleaned my room. It had been a year since I had joined office. That day I decided to clean my room.

So, I was 25, jobless, had no girlfriend and according to Shilpa fused with Jane Austin, the chances of me falling in love, or being able to get a girlfriend are falling at an incredibly accelerating rate. I would most probably end up having an arranged marriage, which would end up in a divorce. But wait a minute; I would not be able to have an arranged marriage, as I will never be able to get another job! My boss who I must have left soo furious at me, for saying all the things that I said, would make sure that no other architect ever hires me, or gives me any kind of a job! It is a very small world for architects and everyone knows everyone. So my boss can completely make sure of that. So no parent would marry their daughter to me – a jobless architect. So my life, it was completely, officially over.

That was what I was thinking, when my phone rang.

O MY GOD IT WAS RUSHI! O MY GOD! I WAS 5:30 P.M! GOD! WHAT WAS I THINKING! OR DOING FOR THAT MATTER! I WAS LATE!!

I become a ricksahw puller.

I could not believe it! I had the golden chance of spending one full hour with Rushi and making my fourth proposal actually larger than life. AND I WAS LATE! I picked my bag and rushed out! 'RICKSHAW!' I called out loud. There was only one *rikshaw wala* on the road, an old, tired, gray haired *rikshaw wala*.

"Park Plaza." I told him in a hurry.

"*Bees rupaye lagenge saab.*" He said.

"*Arre aap sau le lena! Please Zara jalhi Chaliye.*"

I could not believe it! It was 5:45 already. Rushi was to leave in another fifteen minutes! The old *ricshaw wala* kept peddling, slowly and slowly and slowly.

My phone started to ring again.

"Hey! Rushi, I am gonna be there in another five minutes." I said.

"Ok, make it fast yaar, my taxi is already here."

"Don't worry, I will be there in a jiffy!" I said.

In a jiffy! At the rate the *ricksaw wala* was peddling, I could not have reached there in a thousand years! Every other vehicle was going vroom past us!

"Uncle, *kya mai rickshaw chala sakta hoon?*"

"*Hainnn? Kayaaaa?*"

"Please uncle, *bahut zaroori hai, ... mera jaldi pahunchna!*"

"*Theek hai beta aajao.*"

He slowly got off the peddling seat, and I quickly I got on to it. He slowly settled down on the passenger seat, and then, beep beeeeeep, beep beeeeep, all the cars honked on the road as I struggled to carve my way through the traffic, like a snake, at full speed.

5:55, and I was there. I got off the *rickshw*, handed the money to the old man, turned around, panting. There she was, in a wonderful, light pink flowery dress. I ran to her, and stood there, trying to catch my breath.

"Its ok, relax, lets go and sit on that bench." She pointed at a bench in the small garden of the hotel.

She took a flask out of her bag and handed me water in a cup. I drank it, closed my eyes and rested my head back on the bench, smiling.

I opened my eyes and saw the clouds in the sky. "Do you still see the clouds ..."

"The way I used to back then? Yes." She interrupted me.

"See over there, can you see? Can you see a Raj? Bent down on his knee? And there, a Rushi, right in front of him?"

Rushi smiled.

"With his heart in his hands, he is offering his heart to her. For life." I said

Rushi was looking up, staring in the sky.

"There next to that puppy." I said pointing at the two human like cottony fluffy white figures in the sky.

She turned around and looked at me.

"I have a present for you." I took out a red rose and the red diary in which I had written all my feeling for Rushi since the first day I saw her. I had wrapped it with a red wrapping paper and had tied it with a pink ribbon and a nice bow on top.

"This is something that I had always kept with me. But it always belonged to you. These are my feelings for you."

"Raj " she tried to say something, but I stopped her.

"You don't have to say anything. I am not asking for an answer.

This is nothing new, which would change anything. This has always been there, all this time."

Beep Beep, the taxi that was waiting for her began to honk.

She got up, and hugged me.

"Raj, I will call you when I get back." She said.

"Ok."

We walked to the taxi. She sat in it, like an angel, holding her dress, and setting it properly as she sat.

The engine roared. She waved. I waved back. The car began to move; leaving small clouds of dust behind. And slowly and slowly and slowly, vanished, out of my sight. And I stood there, waving in that direction.*

---

* What? Was that it? Was this what I was running away from all my life? Or running after??!!

Epilogue

I say good-bye.

That's it. This is where I end my story. What? You want to know what happened next? You want to know what Rushi said when she called me when she got back home? Well, she said what you want her to say. If you want her to say, "I always loved you Raj. But I always wanted you to tell me that in person, standing in front of me, like a man. And now you have done that, I am yours." Well, then she said that.

And if you want her to say, "Raj! You are a jerk. Throughout your life you had never been able to make up your mind who you are actually in love with! You do not deserve me at all." Then she said that. My dear friend, this is a book in which you have your own ending. Here *that* happens what you want.

As far as others are concerned, J.J and Aksha, Deep and Raina are still going strong. And I know as a fact that I will be keeping in touch with all my friends, Guneet, Shalini, Pragya, Prateek, Manisha, everyone.

Maybe its true, what Karan tried to tell the audience in *Kuch Kuch Hota hai*, maybe its only once that we fall in love, maybe it happens only once in life. But if we lose that love, or can't attain it, it does not mean that our life is over. Unrequited love is only the purest, look at any for instance, Romeo and Juliet. *Heer Ranjha, Sohni Mahival* hmm. Cool! May be our story is also like one of these. Hummmm. Uff! What am I talking? It is not true! They *both* loved each other in the same way. But does love have to be like that to be true? Or great? Is one-sided love not as pure or great as two-sided love? Anyways, coming back to the point, life may start with love, but it does not end with the end of love. That, in itself, is a new beginning.

I may or may not be able to get Rushi. She may or may not be mine. But the beautiful moments, the delightful time that I have spent with her, will always be mine. And will always give me happiness. I may not have her in my life in reality, but I will always have her in my dreams. Not even God can take that away from me. No, wait a minute; he can, if he makes me loose my memory. (God! I remember Nicolas Spark's *The Notebook*!* It gives a horrible feeling!) But unless that happens, I will always have her, in my mind, in my heart, just like Jack always stayed with Rose, in *Titanic*.)

I have packed all my bags. I am leaving this city today. It does not have anything more to offer to me. Not in career, not in love. I am moving to Dehradun. Today once again, I am standing on another gateway, which will lead me to a host of new places and people. A new beginning is here again. And I am all set to start everything, all over again. (Now I feel used to it.)

I hope you enjoyed reading my story. And well, if you didn't! You know what to do – throw this book into the dustbin! And warn your entire circle not to read it, even if anyone offers them huge amounts of money. And run frantically away at the sight of my next book, which will soon be out, on the bookshelves, in a bookstore near you! Have a nice day my friends. It was nice meeting you.

---

* or its Indian adaptation – U Me Aur Hum.

Who does not dream of an Oscar speech?. This is mine.

"Ok, now this is the tough part. I hope I don't miss out anyone.

I would start with my family - my Mom, Dad, Anu (she read the whole draft without uttering a word of complaint. She does not read, I think apart from this book, she has not read any!), Chacha ji (cum Mausa ji), chachi ji (cum Mausi ji) for constantly supporting me while I was writing this book as I kept quitting and switching jobs. Eying and peeping into my computer screen every now and then as I wrote and when asked, for saying, 'nothing nothing, I was *toh* was just… you carry on.' My elder sister Lili didi and my Jijaji, who always kept telling me to follow my heart, and to follow it truly. Vani and Gunchi, my 9 and 11 year old niece and nephew for constantly jumping and shrieking with joy for *Mamu* was writing a book that would be sold in bookshops. My dog Brutus, who went blind as I was writing this book and actually taught me how to love someone truly, which was the basic inspiration for this book.

The one who started it all, Anuja Arora – the schoolgirl of today, who I randomly met one day on Orkut. On being asked if she reads books when she is free, she said, 'I never read in my free time, I don't like to study when I am free', rightly overthrowing the idea completely that reading still is, a means of entertainment. (I hope I have succeeded in proving that to her, fingers crossed!) It was she who got me started with this book. It was fun sending her one chapter everyday and see her begging for more.

My friends. Guneet, for helping me shape the characters better and constantly giving the strongest criticism. Shalini, for spooning me with all the encouragement on earth. Shilpa, for always being there and constantly telling me that I was doing a great job. Kunal, for all his excitement and encouragement. Shweta for constantly telling me to 'add detail, that is what brings it to life. That is where all the beauty lies' Prateek for constantly reminding me to believe in my self and that anything is possible 'when you believe'. Pragya, for always being next to me and never even showing the slightest frown when I irritated and pestered her to read my 'new chapters' every morning! And for forcing me to cut out all the cheesy, vulgar and porny (as she put it) love making scenes, which I used to have great fun writing and reading out. For helping me improve and rephrase the book via chat even when she was in office! Also for telling me that it was *not* the 'best book' she has read, but…she enjoyed being a part. Shruti Soni for helping remove all the dramatic flaws in the story. Priyanka, for her patient presence throughout and reading the whole book part by part as I wrote and sent it to her online. Also for tolerating me all this time when I would talk about only the book and nothing else (this goes for everyone mentioned here by the way.) My sweet office darlings, Raina (*my* Shona), J.J, Deeptimay, Chavi (sorry for have kept you waiting but now you can read the full thing!), Isha and Sid. Thnx for all the help and support [for writing and for assisting me to take all the printouts from office *without letting anyone know*. Sorry Deepa (the office administrator), but it was I who would always finish the toner in the A4 laser printer.] The daily after lunch read-and-discuss sessions are a set of memories that are gonna stay with me forever. Shivani, for taking me to *the ridge* where I kept going time and again (in my book.), and for being so inspiring and compelling me to put more meaning in the book and not makeing like just another F.R.I.E.N.D.S episode.

Aksha for teaching be the basics of gossip science.

Mrs. Bajwa – the best teacher I ever came across, for helping me refine the initial drafts. See ma'am! We did it!

Shobha Sengupta, the owner of the wonderful and cozy bookshop called Quill and Canvas in Galleria DLF IV Gurgaon, for telling me that I had a good manuscript and forcing me to take it to the publishers. "just walk in with the manuscript" she would always say.

O god! I am running out of time; please stop the music, just 30 seconds more.

My ladlords, Naveen Bhaiya and Sheena didi for being so considerate and saying, '*Koi baat nahi* Rahul, pay us next month.' When I never had money to pay the rent and wandered unemployed.

Special thanx to my eversweet publisher and everyone at Strishti publishers and distributors for believing in me. And my editor for giving me a new perspective and helping me refine the language.

All my friends, Rinku, Shipra, Varun, Rashim didi, ...o my god! I hope I am not forgetting anyone! ...Ayodh, Tanu, Chiranjeet aunty (for all the special cakes and meals and reassuring me that I was doing a great job.), Abhaya, Deepika, Toshika, Superna Dutta Mehta, I.P (Inderpreet Bhutani), for being around to read help.

Cecilia Ahern and Sophie Kinsella for writing such wonderful books that made me want to write!

All my friends for letting me use their names and allowing me to cook up all the stories on earth.

All those innocent people who had to go through the agony of listening me talk when I caught hold of them in the malls or on the roadsides or in trains or buses where they would be relaxing or strolling or just...traveling, and eat their heads up talking about my book.

And last but not the least, my online Internet friends and critics, Amit Taneja and Devika Arora, Rahul Sharma, Sabby (and the rest of my team of 'unknown' internet friends and critics) for their constant help and support.

And everyone who I have ever known or come across, all of them have been an influence.

I didn't write this book alone. All the people mentioned here, we all did.

OK FINE I LEAVE, KEEP THE MUSIC LOW. BUT BEFORE I LEAVE I MUST TELL YOU… GOD! KEEP THE MUSIC LOW! ALL THE CHARACTERS AND INCIDENTS IN THIS BOOK ARE COMPLETELY A PIECE OF FICTION AND ANY RESEMBLANCE WITH ANY EVENT OR PERSON LIVING OR DEAD IS PURELY COINCIDENTAL.

THANK YOU ALL! O! LADIES AND GENTLEMEN, THANK YOU LADIES AND GENTLEMEN!! HAVE A WONDERFUL NIGHT! AND WHOOPY, YOU ARE DOING A GREAT JOB! **THANK YOU!**

(Loud music plays as I walk down the steps.)